Reason To Live

David Homick

Reason to Live
Copyright © 2018 David Homick
All rights reserved

Published by Blue Knight Media
ISBN 978-0-9906126-5-0

Cover design by David Homick

This book or any portion thereof may not be reproduced or used in any
manner whatsoever without the express written permission of the
publisher or author except for use of brief quotations in a book review.
Your support of the author's rights is appreciated.

The characters, incidents and dialogs in this book are fictional and are not
to be construed as real. Any resemblance to actual events or persons,
living or dead, is purely coincidental.

"It's never too late to be what you might have been."
~ George Eliot

CHAPTER **ONE**

Richard Dunham watched the ICU nurse push buttons on the bedside monitor. He had only been awake for a few hours. He set an empty Jello cup on the tray table and licked the plastic spoon.

"Can I get another one of those?"

She turned.

He held up the empty cup.

"Sure. As soon as I—"

"And a cheeseburger."

She smiled. "Let's not get ahead of ourselves. You can't just jump back in with both feet."

He set the cup down and stared at his hand like he'd never seen it before.

The nurse picked up the empty cup and watched Richard shake his head. "What's the matter?"

Doctor Howard entered the room, wearing a white lab coat and a stern look. He glanced up from the chart in his hand and scratched the graying hair at his temple.

He pushed his glasses up the bridge of his nose with an index finger. "Welcome back."

An uncertain smile flickered on Richard's face.

"How are we feeling?"

"I can't speak for you, Doc, but I've had better days." Richard frowned and straightened the plastic band on his wrist as the doctor walked toward the monitors.

"That's certainly understandable." He studied the screen, then wrote something in the chart.

Richard continued to play with his wrist band. "Who is Michael... Riordan?"

The doctor stopped and turned to Richard with a confused look. "What do you mean?"

He held up his wrist. "I mean my name isn't Michael."

Dr. Howard and the nurse exchanged a questioning glance. "You've been in a coma for two weeks." He reviewed the chart. "It appears there's been some memory loss from your head trauma."

Richard stared ahead, his mind blank, his life up to this point an empty page.

"Michael?" The doctor waited for Richard's attention to return. "What do you remember?"

"Enough to know my name isn't Michael."

Dr. Howard stared over the rim of his glasses. "So, what should I call you?"

"You can call me by my real name. Richard... Richard Dunham."

"Your name is Richard, not Michael?"

"Yes. And I'd appreciate it if you could get me a new one of these." He thrust his wrist toward the doctor.

"I'll see what I can do." More chart writing. "What can you tell me about Richard?"

"Apparently, he likes green Jello," Richard replied, his frustration growing.

"And cheeseburgers," the nurse added.

Doctor Howard glanced at the nurse and forced a smile. "I see." He turned to Richard, his expression as sterile as the room. "I'll schedule an MRI. In the meantime, we'll see about getting you unhooked from all of this equipment and moved to your own room."

Richard shifted his weight uncomfortably. He'd heard of hospitals switching babies, but never full-grown men.

The doctor patted Richard's forearm. "You just relax and take it slow. I'll come by and check on you in a few hours."

Easy for you to say, Richard thought. He watched Dr. Howard speak with the nurse before leaving, their voices too low for him to hear.

"What was that about," he asked the nurse when they were alone.

She smiled. "You should get some rest."

"Rest? I've had plenty of rest."

"Do you want me to get you more Jello?"

He shook his head. "I just lost my appetite."

"Something to drink?"

"Can you help me get to the bathroom?"

"I'm sorry. You can't leave the bed. You're still hooked up to everything."

"What if I have to pee?"

"You have a catheter."

Richard peeked under the sheet. "What if I have to—"

"I'll get you a bed pan."

"That sounds like fun." He closed his eyes. "Never mind."

"I'm sorry, Mr. Riordan, but I—"

"Please don't call me that."

Her expression fell. "Michael, then?"

"Or that." Richard exhaled sharply. "Can you get me a mirror?"

"What for?"

"So I can shave."

Confusion washed over her face. "Are you serious?"

"No. Just get me something that resembles a mirror." He paused. "Please?"

"Let me see what I can do," she said before leaving the room.

Richard tried to keep his wits about him, but his confusion, which had turned to fear, teetered on the verge of panic. He needed a drink. Whiskey. Straight up. In a vase. Given his present situation, he didn't think it an unreasonable request. He pushed the tray table away from the bed and sent a cup of ice chips skittering across the floor.

The nurse returned in time to witness his tantrum. "Mr. Riordan!"

"I thought I asked you not to call me that."

She took a deep breath. "I found a mirror."

Richard snatched it from her hand and held it in front of his face.

"This is a joke, right?" He stared at an unfamiliar face in the small mirror. The man that looked back appeared similar in age, perhaps a few years older than his forty-four years. He turned his head from side to side. The stranger did the same. "I gotta hand it to you, it's a good one. How did you do it?"

"Do what?"

He held up the mirror and examined both sides of it. He belched out a nervous laugh. "Seriously. How did you do it?"

She blinked a few times. "I don't know what you're talking about."

"Come over here." He pointed to the side of the bed.

The nurse hesitated before taking a step.

Richard held the mirror away from them with one hand and pulled her closer with the other. She resisted.

"I'm not going to bite. I need you to look in the mirror."

Her muscles relaxed, and she leaned in closer.

Richard held up the mirror. Two faces looked back, neither of them his. He no longer teetered on the verge of panic. He swam in a pool of it.

He turned to her. "You look the same."

"So do you. It's a mirror." She made no attempt to hide her confusion. "I don't understand."

Richard handed her the mirror. "That makes two of us."

"I'm sorry, Mr. Rior—" She pulled away. "I'm sorry. I have to get back to the station."

He called after her as she walked out the door. "What the hell's going on here?"

She disappeared without a reply.

Richard closed his eyes and settled back onto the pillow. He tried to reassure himself that this was only a dream. A bad dream. Or perhaps he'd not yet woken up from the coma. Who knew what went on in a comatose mind?

When he opened his eyes, a short, gray-haired man in hospital scrubs stood in the doorway. After a moment, the man spoke.

"Richard?"

He bolted upright in bed and grabbed his head with both hands. He studied the man through squinted eyes. "You know who I am?"

"We need to talk."

CHAPTER **TWO**

Richard scratched the bandages on his head, and watched the gray-haired man walk over to the doctor's stool and sit. He didn't recognize him, but what little memory he had was suspect.

The man glanced at the door as he wheeled closer to the bed.

"You know who I am." Relief mixed with hope grabbed hold of Richard's breath.

"I know who you *were*," the stranger replied.

Richard exhaled. "What does that mean?"

"It's complicated."

"How about if you try to *uncomplicate* it for me?" He shook his head to clear it. "Who are you?"

"My name is Arthur."

"The nurse is in on this too, isn't she? Who put you up to this?"

"You think I erased your memory?"

Richard glanced at the IV bag hanging above his bed. "You could have put something in there, I guess."

"I could have."

"Maybe your real name isn't Arthur. Maybe that's a CIA code name."

Arthur smiled. "Maybe your real name isn't Richard."

"That seems to be the general consensus around here."

Arthur placed his hand on Richard's forearm. "I'm here to help you."

Richard studied the stranger, unsure of his motives. Arthur was the only person he'd met who knew his real name. That had to count for something. "And just how do you think you can help me?"

"First, you need to understand that you are now Michael Riordan."

Richard pulled his arm away. "No, I'm not."

"Yes, you are."

"I may not be able to remember much, but I know my own name."

"Repeat after me, my name is Michael—"

"What part of NO don't you understand?"

He gave Michael a stern look. "This isn't a game."

"Yeah, more like I died and went to hell."

"That would only be half right."

Arthur stood and pulled down the sheet to expose Michael's legs.

"What are you doing?"

The odd little man rubbed his palms together, then held them about six inches apart momentarily before extending them an inch or two above Michael's exposed legs. Arthur moved his hands slowly up one leg then down the other.

"You could have at least bought me dinner first," Michael quipped.

"Shhh."

When he finished, he pulled the sheet back up.

"What the hell was that?"

"It's called Reconnective Healing. It will reduce your recovery time."

Michael leaned forward toward Arthur. "How about you do my head next."

Arthur smiled. "It doesn't work like that."

Michael closed his eyes and dropped onto the pillow. "Now what?"

Arthur pulled a photo of a man and a woman from his pocket and showed it to Michael when he opened his eyes.

"Do you know these people?"

"A few minutes ago, I would have said the one on the left was me, but now, I don't know what I know."

"And the woman?"

Michael shrugged. "So, tell me what happened... and why does everyone..." He paused. "Who is Michael?"

"Richard had an auto accident. Michael was the other driver. He ended up in a coma, and well, here you are."

"Here who is?"

"You're a walk-in. You have a new identity."

"What?"

"The accident was fatal for Richard, but he wasn't ready to leave."

"Is anybody ever ready?"

"Unfinished business, you called it."

Michael closed his eyes and squeezed the bridge of his nose as a few seconds passed. "Let me get this straight. I'm me, but I'm not me?"

Arthur smiled. "Now, we're getting somewhere."

A nurse entered the room and stopped when she noticed Arthur. "I'm sorry, I didn't know anyone was in here."

Arthur froze for a moment, then stood and picked up a stethoscope from the table. He hung it around his neck. "No worries. I was just leaving."

"You must be new here," she said.

"I am," Arthur responded on his way to the door. "Doctor Mulligan," he added. "Please, carry on."

An orderly arrived as soon as Arthur left. The nurse announced they would move Michael to a private room on the fourth floor.

With the transfer complete, the nurse left Michael—or Richard, or whoever he was—alone to think in his new private room. He wondered who paid for his privacy. Who was Michael Riordan? What was his story? That is, if he even believed what Arthur had told him. He needed time to sort things out, but he had very little to work with—an auto accident, a coma, a strange little man who appears to be the only one who knows his real name. He stared at the ceiling desperately trying to unearth a memory, anything that might shed some light on who he is, was, or how he got to this place.

He needed to get to the bottom of this, and he had to do it sooner rather than later. The pain wasn't as bad as he'd anticipated when he swung the first leg over the side of the bed. The second leg became tangled in the catheter tube.

"I wouldn't do that if I were you."

Michael froze. A tall, forty-something woman stood in the doorway. Her muscular arms strained the sleeves of her navy-blue scrubs.

She continued in a thick German accent. "You won't be camping happy if tube pulls out."

Michael stopped and forced a smile. "You mean happy camper?"

She nodded. "Time for physical therapy."

"Now?"

Arthur appeared beside her in the hall.

"Am I glad to see you," Michael blurted. "Get in here."

The therapist took a step forward and blocked his path.

Michael panicked. "I need to talk to him."

She looked at Arthur like she might reach down and put him in a headlock, then turned to Michael. "Catheter can't come out until you can walk to the bathroom on your own." She folded her beefy arms across her chest.

"A couple of minutes won't matter, will it?"

She glared, then spoke reminiscent of a scene from *The Terminator*. "I'll be back."

Arthur entered the room as she turned and walked away.

"Is it just me?" Michael asked, "Or does she remind you of—"

"That's good." Arthur smiled. "A memory."

Michael shrugged. "Yeah, great. I remember my name and a thirty-year-old movie. What happens when I get out of here? I don't know where to go or what to do. You're going to help me, right?"

"Richard once told me he didn't need my help."

Michael threw his arms in the air. "Do I look like Richard?"

"There's only so much I can do."

"I find that hard to believe, after what you did down there." Michael pointed to his legs.

Arthur smiled and handed Michael the photo he'd shown him earlier.

"Where'd you get this?"

"Richard had it in his pocket."

"How did *you* get it?"

"That's not important," Arthur said with a dismissing wave of his hand. "What's important is the woman in the photo."

Michael studied the photo. "Who is she?"

"She's your unfinished business."

Nurse *Schwarzenegger* returned. She glared at Arthur, and he fled the room. She helped Michael out of bed and steadied him as he took his first steps in almost a month. The intensity of the pain in his muscles and joints surprised him, and he managed only a few steps before he returned to bed. Michael needed to accept the fact that it might be a while before he was back to his old self—whoever that was.

CHAPTER **THREE**

Two days later, Michael moved about the room on his own, no longer tethered to his bed. He grew impatient with Arthur, who hadn't returned since the physical therapist chased him away. His recovery had moved along quicker than anyone had expected, and Michael wondered if his progress had anything to do with Arthur's magic hands. He walked to the bathroom where he stared into the mirror at an unfamiliar face.

"Who the hell are you?" he whispered.

The reflection blurred. Michael blinked, and the face became Richard's.

The bathroom changed. His surroundings were strange but somehow familiar. He raked his hands back through his hair before he turned off the light and opened the door. Darkness filled the hall.

The woman from Arthur's photo stood a few feet away with her arms folded. "Where have you been?"

Richard shook off his surprise and brushed past her. "I'm tired. Can we do this in the morning?" He climbed into bed.

She followed him into the guest bedroom. "You won't be here in the morning!" She grabbed the comforter and yanked it off the bed.

"Where am I supposed to go at this hour?"

"You can go to hell for all I care." She exhaled sharply. "I'm sure your girlfriend would be happy to put you up for the night."

"My what?"

She picked up a small, framed photo from the dresser and threw it in his direction. "Move it!"

Glass shattered. The photo that Arthur had shown Michael stared at him through the shards. Emily, he thought. Her name is Emily.

Michael squeezed his eyes shut. He opened them to find himself back in the hospital bathroom. Beads of sweat had formed on his forehead, and he splashed cold water on his face.

Too restless to return to his bed, he peeked his head out of his room. Michael shuffled toward the empty nurses' station and ducked inside unnoticed. He glanced down the hall from time to time while he rifled through a stack of charts on the desk. A high-back office chair in the corner of the station turned around slowly.

"You won't find what you're looking for in there," Arthur said calmly.

Michael jumped. "Jeezus, Arthur. You trying to put me back in a coma?"

He stood and shook his head. "I hoped you'd remember more, but memory loss is not that uncommon with walk-ins."

"There's that word again."

A nurse stepped out of a room at the end of the hall.

"Let's go for a walk," Arthur said, "before you get us both in trouble."

Michael followed Arthur down the hall. He grabbed his arm. "What the hell is a walk-in?"

Arthur's eyes drifted for a moment. "A walk-in can happen when one soul who wishes to leave, in this case Michael, makes an agreement with another who wishes to return, in this case Richard. One walks in as the other walks out, so to speak."

"I did that?" Michael scratched his temple.

"You hurt someone, and you wanted a chance to make things right."

"Emily?"

"You are kindred spirits, traveling together through many lifetimes." Arthur smiled before his expression fell. "I'm afraid this is not the first time you've broken her heart."

"Really?"

"It's a pattern. One you've been unable to break, so you try again and again."

"You mean we're stuck because of me?"

"Let's just say the two of you had agreed to help each other on your journeys. She won't bail on you just because it hasn't been going well lately. It's called unconditional love."

"What can I do?"

"You're doing it," Arthur reminded him. "Perhaps you don't remember, but we had a conversation in the hospital shortly after you died. In fact, we talked about some of the same things we're talking about here. You made up your mind that the cycle would end with this lifetime."

Confusion clouded Michael's thoughts.

Arthur rubbed his chin. "Ironic how you always seem to come to that conclusion after you die."

"So, what happened?" Michael asked.

"My job was to assist you with your transition, but you refused to go. You put up a pretty big stink, as I recall."

Michael remained silent.

"I was moved by your devotion to her, so I interceded on your behalf."

"I guess I should thank you."

"You were offered a second chance, but there was a logistical problem. You were already dead. So, together, we came up with a plan."

"A walk-in." Michael nodded. The past few days made a little more sense.

"Yes. You couldn't come back the usual way. There wasn't enough time. This was the only way to get you back here and maintain a reasonable age differential. Fortunately, we found an appropriate donor."

"This wasn't a hostile takeover, was it?"

"Oh, no. It's always a mutual agreement."

Michael slowed as they approached his room. "So, what's the rest of the plan?"

Arthur smiled. "You'll have to figure that out on your own."

Michael stared at Arthur, feeling somewhat deflated. "But how am I—"

"You've been given the gift of a new perspective and a chance to make different choices. What you do with it is up to you."

"No pressure there," Michael said wryly.

Arthur placed a hand on Michael's shoulder when they reached the door. "Just follow your heart, my friend."

"Are you coming in?"

"It looks like you have company," Arthur said with a smile.

A woman in a tie dye t-shirt and faded jeans stared out the window on the far side of the room. She turned when Michael entered.

"Can I help you?" he asked.

The woman frowned. "*Can I help you?*" She ran to Michael and wrapped her arms around him.

CHAPTER **FOUR**

The woman held on for an awkward moment. Michael shifted his weight for balance, unsure what to do with his hands. He reluctantly patted her back. She stood nearly a foot shorter than he, and somehow felt familiar in his arms. Her sandy blonde hair had a slight wave and was layered to just below her ears. She appeared low-maintenance; the type that could get out of bed in the morning, run her fingers through her hair, and be good-to-go. It worked for her.

"God, Michael, I was afraid I'd never get to do this again." She released him and punched his arm. "That's for scaring the crap out of me."

"And you are...?"

"You big dope. Angie? Your favorite sister?" She shook her head. "Jesus Christ, Michael. You really don't remember me?"

"Nothing personal." He took a few steps toward the bed. "How many sisters do I have?"

"Just me." She gave him a wary glance then a smile. "You couldn't handle any more."

He climbed into bed with a slight grimace of pain.

"When are they going to release you?" she asked.

"I don't know. When they do, can you give me a ride home... wherever that is?"

Angie studied Michael with a worried look, and he shifted uncomfortably in his bed.

"Who are these people?" she asked when she noticed the photo on the bedside table.

Michael hesitated.

Angie looked around the room nervously. "Are we in the right room?"

I wish it were that simple. He pointed to the bandage on his head. "You're asking me?" Michael smiled. "Relax. This is my room. The picture is just some old friends that stopped by."

Angie studied him through squinted eyes, then shook her head. She pulled a notebook and pen from her purse. "They warned me about the memory thing. Maybe this will help. You can write things down as you remember them."

"You're assuming I remember how to write."

Michael watched Angie set the notebook down on the table. It fell off the edge and hit the floor with a *thud.*

The noise brought back a memory. A dreadful one.

The front door had just slammed behind him with a thud. Richard stood on a porch. Emily had woken him and thrown him out of his own house. He hesitated a moment, then tried the doorknob.

"Unlock the door..." he urged. "Please?"

"Happy Anniversary, Richard," Emily replied sarcastically from inside.

Anniversary? Richard squeezed his eyes shut for a moment. "I'm sorry, Em. I..."

He tried the doorknob again. After a few moments of silence, Richard turned to leave. At the edge of the porch, he looked over his shoulder. "Don't forget to feed Bogey."

Michael stared blankly, lost in thought.

Angie picked up the notebook and set it back on the table. "Earth to Michael..."

Michael pulled the sheet up to his neck. "You need to go."

"Are you kidding me? I just got here."

"Doctor says I need rest."

Angie glared for a moment, then threw her purse over her shoulder. "Good to see you, too."

Michael chewed his bottom lip as he watched her leave. He needed time alone to process his disturbing memories.

Michael wore a frown in bed, praying that the next memory might shed a more positive light on Richard's past. A perky, young nurse entered the room and stood by his bed.

"I thought you'd be in better spirits after getting rid of the bag," she said.

Michael turned and acknowledged her presence. "My sister?"

"What?"

"She was just trying to help. I shouldn't have snapped like that, but I—"

"No. I meant the catheter."

"Oh." He shook his head to clear it, then paused for a moment. "Have you ever had a flashback of something that you don't remember ever happening? I mean, that's crazy right?" He waited for something—anything—that might help explain what he'd experienced.

"It's not that crazy, I guess, given your condition." She forced a smile. "The doctor thinks it's only temporary. Anything you remember is a good sign."

Michael nodded, unable to explain the fact that the memories didn't belong to the man she looked at, but to the other guy. The stowaway inside.

Doctor Howard entered the room and nodded to the nurse. He turned to Michael. "Feeling any better today?"

Arthur had told him that if he didn't lighten up and play along, he could be stuck here for a while. *Showtime!* He grinned. "Much better, Doc. When do you think I might go home?"

He picked up the chart and studied it. "Your MRI results show nothing abnormal or suspicious, but I'm still concerned about your memory loss."

"My memory's fine. No problem there. Go on, ask me anything."

"Okay." He paused. "If your memory is working again, surely you must know your name."

"Of course I do. It's Michael Riordan… and stop calling me Shirley."

The doctor laughed. "Well, it seems you've developed a sense of humor since I last saw you." He wrote something on the chart. "That's a good sign."

"Well?" Michael asked.

"Where are we?"

"St. Mark's Hospital."

"Why?"

"I had a car accident."

"When?"

"About a month ago."

More chart writing.

"Can I go home now?"

"Where is that?"

"Uh…" Michael hesitated. "It's here in Springfield."

The doctor waited. He pushed his glasses up and studied Michael.

"1611 Magnolia Terrace," he offered, grateful that Angie had written his name and address in the notebook as if he were a child on the first day of school. "Do you need the zip?"

"I think that'll be sufficient." He wrote in the chart again before standing. "I'll sign the discharge papers, and you can be on your way tomorrow."

"Thanks, Doc."

Michael watched him leave with mixed feelings. The hospital had been a safe haven. Tomorrow, he would step out into a world he knew nothing about.

CHAPTER **FIVE**

Now that Michael felt better, hospital food had lost its appeal. Funny how not having eaten for nearly a month lowers one's culinary standards. He didn't finish tonight's mystery meat, and for the record, Jello is not a proper dessert. A big piece of pie with a side of ice cream—now, that's dessert!

Michael wandered into the empty cafeteria just before closing time. He bought a cup of coffee and a slice of blueberry pie a la mode—a well-deserved treat on his last night in captivity. He set them down on an empty table next to his notebook and photo.

Michael devoured half of the pie while he studied the photo. He wondered how that pretty face held such mystery and somehow felt familiar at the same time. He took a sip of coffee as he stared into those green eyes.

Arthur scanned the room from the doorway. Their eyes met and he walked in Michael's direction.

The room faded, replaced by a streetscape.

The night air hung heavy like a warm, wet blanket. Richard leaned against his car, parked in front of the Lighthouse Homeless Shelter, and watched his friend Marshawn James through the office window. Two years ago, MJ had been a client and Richard a volunteer. Now, MJ worked the overnight shift, giving back to the organization that offered him a second chance after a stretch in prison. Tonight, their former roles would be reversed.

Richard crossed his arms and leaned back against his car. He watched a strange little man with feral, gray hair drag a suitcase along the sidewalk. The man slowed as he approached the car, his breath labored.

"Are you all right?" Richard asked.

A twinkle in the old man's eyes belied his down-and-out appearance. He shook his head, then pulled a handkerchief from his pocket and wiped his neck and forehead. "I need a place to stay tonight."

"What about here?" Richard pointed to the building. "I used to volunteer. I'm sure I could get you a bed."

"That sounds perfect."

Richard reached for the old man's bag.

"Thank you, Richard."

Richard froze and looked up through squinted eyes. "What did you just say?"

"I believe I said thank you."

"No, after that. How do you know my name?"

"What did I say?"

Richard thought for a moment, shook his head, then extended his hand. "I'm Richard Dunham."

"Arthur. Arthur Mulligan."

Richard led the way up the stone steps and into the building.

MJ ushered them into the office. A large man of African-American descent, his shirtsleeves had been removed to accommodate his massive upper arms. He could have been a bouncer or played linebacker for any NFL team. His broad smile, punctuated by a wide gap between his two front teeth, offset his otherwise imposing presence.

Richard explained how he happened to meet Arthur out front, and that they both needed a place to stay for the night.

The big man raised an eyebrow. "Both of you?"

Richard shrugged.

MJ ran a hand over the top of his smooth head. He smiled and led Arthur to the chair beside his desk. "Let's take care of some paperwork so we can get you boys settled for the night."

Richard sat in the corner of the room and studied Arthur, who listened intently to the shelter's rules and procedures. The man's coarse gray hair stuck out in all directions, reminding him of pictures he'd seen of Albert Einstein. His clean, thrift-store clothes contrasted with his otherwise disheveled appearance, and a little twinkle in his soft blue eyes gave Richard the distinct impression there was more to this stranger than his appearance suggested.

MJ ushered Arthur into the living room to wait until he got a bed ready. When he returned, he looked at Richard. "So, my friend, what are we supposed to do with you?"

"I just need a place to crash for the night." He raised an eyebrow. "Can we skip the paperwork?"

MJ grinned and nodded. "You know how I hate paperwork."

"I can stay in the overflow room on the third floor. No one has to know."

"Okay." He hesitated. "But… we were full before you guys showed up tonight, so I'll have to put Arthur in there with you."

"Fine. He's a little strange, but I guess since I'm the one who brought him in, I shouldn't be complaining, right?"

MJ smiled. "The guy looks beat. He'll probably go right to sleep."

Richard stared at a photo of the director and his wife on the desk. "I hope you're right. It's been a rough day."

"What happened, Richard?" MJ's expression turned serious. "Why are you here?"

Richard looked up and sighed. "It's a long story, and even if I understood it, right now I don't have the strength to tell it."

MJ tilted his head. "Are you okay?"

"I'll be fine. I just need to get some sleep."

"Okay then, let's get you two settled."

Neither of them noticed Arthur, who watched from just outside the doorway.

MJ showed them to their room. After they'd settled in and the light had been extinguished, Richard clasped his hands behind his head in his small bed and stared in the direction of the ceiling.

Arthur's voice cut through the darkness. "So, what are you in for?"

"My wife, Emily, got her panties in a bunch because I forgot our anniversary."

"Do you still love her?"

"What kind of question is that? Of course I love her."

"Then, what's the problem?"

Richard pushed himself up on his elbows and turned in Arthur's direction. "For starters, we're having this conversation in a homeless shelter."

"Perhaps there's more to it than a forgotten anniversary."

"Thank you, Doctor Phil."

"You say you love her. How often do you tell her? Or show her?"

An awkward silence sat between them.

"I'm tired. Maybe we can finish this conversation... never."

"It's pretty arrogant to believe we always have tomorrow."

"Just let it go, old man."

"You're about to throw it all away, my friend."

"I'm not your friend. I don't know who you are or what you think you know, but I don't need your help."

The hospital cafeteria came back into focus. Michael shook his head to clear it. Funny how his memory worked just fine inside his flashbacks. Outside, not so much. MJ, the shelter, or the funny little man he met outside had meant nothing five minutes ago.

Arthur approached his table, and Michael motioned for him to sit. Another piece of the puzzle had fallen into place

CHAPTER **SIX**

"Dining out, I see." Arthur took a seat.

"It's the strangest thing." Michael shook his head. "I never liked blueberries."

"Yes, well, it appears Richard and Michael had differing opinions about blueberries."

Michael wondered what other surprises his bizarre circumstance held.

Arthur rested his elbows on the table. "I hear you're going to be released tomorrow."

"Having the *Terminator* for a therapist can be a real motivator." Michael sipped his coffee and studied Arthur. He set the cup down slowly. "I remember you now. We met outside the homeless shelter."

"Indeed, we did."

"As I recall, you were a real pain in the ass." Michael smiled and deposited the last bite of pie into his mouth.

"Well, as far as the pain?" Arthur smiled. "Sometimes the truth hurts."

"I don't know what the truth is anymore." He shrugged. "I've been seeing scenes with people and places that look familiar, but..."

"That's a good sign. They're memories."

"I don't like what I'm seeing."

Arthur remained silent.

Michael tapped the photo. "She's somehow involved in all of it."

"Emily was your wife." Arthur folded his hands on the table. "Your unfinished business."

Michael studied the photo for a moment. "What do you know about her?"

"I know she loved you, but you were about to throw it all away. An adjustment needed to be made."

"An adjustment?"

"Think of it as a second chance."

"Wait… the accident? You did that? Who are you?"

"I'm just a messenger."

"What's that supposed to mean? Who do you work for?"

Arthur stood to leave. "I've said too much already."

"Wait! Who is Michael Riordan? What does he do? Why do so many people here know him?" His eyes pleaded with Arthur for more information. "I need some answers before I'm discharged."

"You wrote a bestseller." Arthur offered a proud smile. "You're something of a celebrity."

"I guess I could have done worse." Michael's expression fell. "But… what do I do now?"

Arthur rested his hand on Michael's shoulder. "Like I told you, you're going to have to figure some things out on your own."

Michael, a bit deflated, lifted his cup to his lips as he watched Arthur leave. He set it down quickly when he realized it was empty. He picked up a pen and began to write.

The next morning, Michael studied himself in the bathroom mirror. He turned his head from side to side. His new skin appeared tanned and more weathered than Richard's, and the stubble on his face seemed to grow twice as fast. He tilted his head back and rubbed his chin, then leaned forward to stare into clear blue eyes. Salt and pepper hair fell across his forehead, grayer than Richard's and a couple inches longer.

Richard was no slouch in the looks department, but Michael Riordan clearly had an advantage on the one-to-ten scale. While it still unnerved him to see someone else's reflection in the mirror, he wondered how Emily would feel about this new facade.

"So, what are you going to do now, handsome?" he said aloud to his reflection in an attempt to make the best of an impossible situation. He waited for an answer that never came.

"Michael?"

"In here."

"I talked to the warden. You're free to go."

"Did you bring some clothes?"

Angie tossed a small overnight bag on the bed. "Let's get out of here before you do something stupid and they change their mind."

Michael watched, eyes wide, from the passenger side while Angie drove his BMW 440i convertible down a winding, tree-lined street in an upper-class neighborhood. Some of the properties were gated, while others showed off their manicured lawns and magazine-worthy landscaping. They turned into the drive of a large Tudor and waited for the garage door to rumble up the rails.

"I live *here?*"

"We both do." The car came to a stop inside the garage. "You let me stay in the guest house out back." She turned to Michael. "Rent-free, in case you forgot."

They exited the car into a spacious garage. The massive door traveled the last few inches and gently came to rest on the concrete floor.

"Always keep the car in the garage. That way, nobody knows you're home."

Michael followed her through a door into the well-appointed kitchen. "Holy…"

He ran his hand along the slab of granite that covered an island the size of Australia. A built-in Sub-Zero refrigerator accounted for nearly half of the back wall. He pulled open one of the massive doors and inspected the contents.

"I don't like pickles," he said.

"Sure you do."

Michael followed her into the living room and lingered to admire the A/V system. Angie waited. He stopped at the baby grand piano.

"Don't get too excited," she warned. "You couldn't carry a tune in a bucket."

Michael turned to her, confused. "What?"

"You tried to learn a couple times, but it didn't stick."

"Who buys a piano like this when they don't play?"

"You haven't seen the basketball court yet."

Michael joined Angie by a set of French doors that opened to a large patio. He stared at the full court in the yard.

"You *had* to have it," Angie reminded him.

"I can't play basketball either?"

"Not anymore. You would have gone pro if you didn't screw up your knee."

Michael looked down at his legs. "Which one? They both hurt."

"Left."

Michael favored his left leg on his way over to a shelf filled with framed photos. He picked up one of the photos. Michael and an attractive woman stood beneath a sign that read Adrianna's Restaurant.

"I think I know this woman."

"Really, Sherlock? What was your first clue?"

An image took shape in his mind. An Italian restaurant. The smell of veal parm and warm garlic bread filled the room.

"Her name is Carolyn," Angie said. "She owns your favorite restaurant."

The doorbell rang, and Angie left Michael staring at the photo. He frowned, and the room morphed into a restaurant.

He sat across from the woman in the photo. Early forties, a real looker with flirtatious eyes. She sipped a glass of wine.

A waiter appeared with menus. Richard leaned back in his chair and watched the candlelight dance in Carolyn's ebony eyes. An air of intimacy surrounded them, their conversation easy. Had they been lovers? The mere thought excited him. But another feeling rose from the pit of his stomach. Something sinister lurked in the shadows, waiting to drag him back to a darker place.

His cell phone rang. He pulled it from his pocket and dismissed Emily's call. "Whoever it is can wait."

Carolyn smiled, apparently pleased with his decision.

He'd have to invent some excuse for being out late. Deceiving Emily was his least favorite part of the whole arrangement, but necessary for the time being.

He sipped his wine and leaned forward. He had a serious matter to discuss. A situation that could bring everything crashing down around him.

"I can't wait any longer," he said.

"We could skip dinner."

"I'm talking about the investment."

Carolyn sighed.

"I want out. I need my money back."

"It's not that easy." She shifted in her chair. "I'm not sure—"

"I borrowed some of that money. If this goes south, I could lose my house."

She sipped her wine. "You can always stay with me."

"I'm serious."

Richard picked up his glass and drank to deflect her coy smile.

"We're so close, Richard." Carolyn placed her hand on Richard's. A smile crept across her lips. "The next time we see each other, we'll be sipping champagne."

Richard let her hand linger, unaware that someone he knew watched from the shadows.

CHAPTER **SEVEN**

Michael looked up from the photo when Angie returned with a tall, well-dressed woman wearing a Hollywood smile.

"Michael, this is Rhonda Williams, your agent."

Rhonda looked at Angie who made a goofy face as she spun her index finger near her temple.

Michael glared at his sister, then turned to Rhonda. "I'm having a little trouble with my memory," he offered.

Rhonda smiled. "Well, it's good to see you back on your feet. We need to talk."

Michael eyed Rhonda suspiciously, then turned to Angie. "This feels like an ambush."

Angie held up her hands. "Michael… just listen to her."

He thought he'd have more time to assimilate his new surroundings and ease into this new life. Apparently, others around him had different ideas.

"No, you listen to me. I just got home from the hospital, for God's sake."

"Michael. Please…"

"Whatever it is can wait," he said over his shoulder on his way outside to the patio.

Michael needed time to sort things out before being thrown back into an unfamiliar job. Seeing that woman, Carolyn, in the picture had unnerved him. She'd obviously meant something to Richard, as well. He needed to know more. Most people who'd suffered a trauma such as his had to rebuild one life; somehow he needed to rebuild two. He picked up a basketball from one of the patio chairs and walked to the court.

The house and the grounds were impressive by any standard. It appeared that Michael didn't cut any corners, something Richard had to do his entire life. He stepped onto the basketball court while the women talked inside.

Michael dribbled the ball for a moment. *Okay, Riordan, let's see what you got.* Despite the soreness in his legs, he attempted a thirty-foot shot. Nothing but net. A smile crept across his lips. He retrieved the ball and took another shot. Another basket. Then another. He dribbled between his legs, spun, and buried a jump shot as Angie walked up alone. Michael turned, grinning from ear to ear.

"What's going on, Michael?"

"Did you see that shot? Richard couldn't have made that if his life depended on it."

"Richard?"

Michael spun the ball on the tip of his finger. "Just an old friend."

"I know you've been through a lot, and I want to help, but you have to—"

"I don't need a lecture, and certainly not from my little sister. What I need is some time."

Neither said anything for a moment.

Finally, Angie folded her arms across her chest. "You have a book signing tomorrow at ten. I told Rhonda you'd be there. I'll drive."

The muscles in his neck tightened and he rolled his head from side to side. "Wanna play a little one-on-one?"

Angie didn't move when Michael passed her the ball. It bounced off her forearm onto the ground.

"C'mon, Ang, don't be such a baby." He retrieved the ball. "I told you, I just need some time."

She fired off a couple of rapid blinks, then held out her hands. Michael passed her the ball again. She caught it, dribbled twice, then heaved it across the yard into the pool before she walked back to the house.

Michael shoved his hands in his pockets and stared at his magnificent house. Sadly, it didn't feel like home. How could it? If this whole charade was his idea as Arthur had suggested, he obviously hadn't thought it through. He needed help from the only other person who knew what was going on.

A neighbor watched from his back yard and offered a wave when their eyes met. Michael returned the gesture. He walked into the house, closed the door, and stood in the middle of the empty room.

"Arthur! Where are you? We need to talk," he said in a hushed voice.

Michael scanned the room, hoping Arthur might suddenly materialize out of thin air. "Okay, you win. I need your help," he said a little louder.

He waited for a response.

"Michael? Are you okay?" Angie called from the other side of the interior door.

"I'm fine. Leave me alone."

Angie opened the door. "Who were you talking to?"

Michael glared. "What part of *leave me alone* don't you understand?"

She hesitated, a hurt look on her face.

Michael said nothing.

Angie held up her middle finger. "This part!" she said and slammed the door.

He'd have to work on that. Like it or not, he needed Angela. Arthur had become too unreliable. Angela, on the other hand, clearly wanted to help with his recovery. And he knew where she lived.

A stranger in a strange land, he needed to rely on their family ties and her intimate knowledge of Michael's life to guide him through this transition period. He planned to use everyone and everything at his disposal to achieve his goal. Which brought him back to Arthur. At the moment, he had no way to contact the strange little man. That would have to change.

Michael picked up the photo of Carolyn from the bookshelf. He stared at her face in an effort to summon another memory. The picture that his memories had painted so far was not a pretty one. If they could be trusted, Richard and Carolyn had been closer than he'd like to admit.

CHAPTER **EIGHT**

Emily sat alone at her favorite table at the Starbucks on Mission Street and watched the traffic through the window. She turned her attention to her own reflection in the glass. Richard hadn't robbed her of everything, she thought. The last few years had taken a toll emotionally, but she looked damn good for her forty-three years. She still had a little sparkle left in those big green eyes.

She picked up her phone and checked the time. Samantha would probably be late for her own funeral. Sam's ex-husband, Matt, had always been the timekeeper in that family. They'd never had children, which Emily knew from experience tended to enforce punctuality. Samantha had divorced Matt five years ago after she caught him cheating. Perhaps not having children had been a blessing.

Emily thought of her daughter, Alexis, and sighed. Would things have turned out differently if she hadn't gotten pregnant? Would Richard have married her anyway? She liked to think so, but recent events have cast a shadow of doubt on everything she once believed.

Lexi had always been *Daddy's Girl* growing up, in spite of, or perhaps because of, Richard's unfortunate relationship with his own father. She had a difficult time dealing with Richard's passing. Emily hated to admit it, but it appeared to have more of an effect on her daughter than herself. Lexi knew nothing of her father's infidelity, and Emily planned to keep it that way.

Richard had been a good father and a decent husband, until he wasn't. Their relationship had been on a downward slide and gaining momentum. She'd wanted to stop it, but she wasn't sure how. They didn't actually fight that much, at least not in the traditional sense. They'd disconnected emotionally, and the space between them grew. Even when there were no obvious signs of trouble, an underlying current of discontent ran just below the surface. She couldn't remember how or when it had started, but it hadn't happened overnight. It was more subtle than that—like a crack in a plaster wall that becomes more pronounced over time.

Emily sipped her first cup, which would usually be gone before Samantha arrived. An elderly couple strolled hand in hand by her window. They appeared to be in their late seventies, perhaps even eighty years old, and she wondered where she and Richard might have been when they reached that age. They had just celebrated their twenty-third wedding anniversary. Well, they would have celebrated it if Richard hadn't forgotten it altogether.

In the past, Richard had been enthusiastic about every anniversary, even when they dated. On their one-month anniversary, he'd brought her a single red rose. Every month after that for the first year, he'd added another rose. After they married, he'd kicked it up a notch, with each year's gift an attempt to outdo the last. Eventually, his enthusiasm had waned, as had the originality of his ideas.

She tried to convince herself that anniversary surprises did not indicate the true measure of a man's love, but she couldn't shake the feeling that they were somehow a barometer for the overall health of a relationship.

Emily scanned the room. Several patrons sat alone, and she wondered if they too might be waiting for a punctually challenged friend or relative. The elderly couple caught her eye again as they disappeared around the corner, much like her plans to grow old with her husband had vanished.

She took a sip of coffee, then stared at her cup as she turned it slowly in her hands. She remembered the day Samantha confirmed her suspicions about Richard's infidelity. She'd been seated at the same table when Sam walked in fifteen minutes late.

"Hi, Em," Sam had said like she was right on time.

"Hey, Sam. Glad you could make it." The sarcasm was lost on Samantha, who never acknowledged her tardiness. Emily wondered if she was even aware of it.

"God, Em, you don't look so good. Are you okay?"

"Thanks for noticing," Emily said with a contrived smile. "I haven't been sleeping well. What's your excuse?"

They fell silent for a moment. They laughed together at Emily's remark before walking to the counter to place their order.

"So, what's been keeping you up at night?" Samantha asked when they'd returned to their seats.

"I'm not sure... I mean, something isn't right, but I don't know exactly what it is."

"You and Richard having trouble again?"

Emily hesitated. "This time it's different. He's distracted all the time—distant—like his body's there, but his mind is somewhere else."

"Maybe that's not such a bad thing. If the sex is good, men don't need to talk all that much. Most of what they say is a load of crap anyway."

Emily looked at Samantha as if she were a misbehaving child. Samantha raised her eyebrows, grinned, and shrugged.

"Last Saturday, he gets up earlier than me and takes a drive to Riverside," Emily said. "What's in Riverside? I ask. Nothing, he says. He stopped and had breakfast. Then last night, he's grilling steaks— and you know how particular he is about that. So, I can hardly believe it when I walk outside and he's staring off into space while the steaks are

on fire. If he'd been standing any closer, he would have gone up in flames with them."

Samantha remained silent for a moment. "Do you think he might have someone else on the side?"

"The thought crossed my mind," Emily admitted, "but…"

Samantha sipped her coffee.

"I asked him last night, and he assured me he didn't."

"Oh, I see. So that means it didn't happen." She exhaled her frustration. "God, Emily, do you know how many times I asked Matt before I caught him with his pants down?"

Emily glanced around and motioned to Samantha to lower her voice.

"Men are cowards," Sam continued in a slightly more subdued manner. "They don't like to admit things like that, and never the first time you ask."

Emily stared out the window until Samantha spoke again.

"I hate to break it to you, Sis, but Richard is just like all the rest of them. In my courtroom, men are guilty until proven innocent. Don't be fooled by—"

"Stop it, Sam. I never should have said anything."

"You didn't have to. I can see it all over your face." Samantha leaned forward. "I'm sorry, Em, but I just don't want to see you get hurt like I did."

"This is nothing like that."

"Isn't it?"

"What does that mean?" Emily's brow furrowed. "Sam… is there something you haven't told me?"

Samantha looked away and shifted in her chair.

Emily raised her voice. "Sam?" Fear rose in her chest and formed a lump in her throat. Sam's obvious discomfort added to the mounting anxiety. Emily swallowed hard. "If you know something, please tell me," she said in a softer voice.

"All right," Samantha said. "I didn't know whether I should say anything."

"Whatever it is, just tell me."

"About three weeks ago, we had a retirement party at Adrianna's Restaurant. I noticed Richard when I passed by one of the dining rooms on the way out. I considered stopping to say hello to my favorite sister when I realized that the attractive, forty-something woman with him wasn't you. So, I ordered a drink and found a spot in the corner where I could watch them."

"Richard has a lot of female clients. I'm sure it was just a business meeting. He's had quite a few lately."

"Business? I'm no expert, Em, but this didn't look like a business meeting."

"What do you mean?"

"Well, besides the empty bottle of wine, they held hands across the table."

"How many drinks had you had at that point?"

"I know what I saw."

"I think, in your mind, you saw Matt, not Richard."

After Matt had cheated on Sam and she'd promptly divorced him, Emily had detected a hint of jealousy from her sister. Sam had become much more sarcastic with her comments, projecting her disdain for her ex onto men in general, and Richard in particular. Richard was nothing like Matt, a fact which must have become painfully obvious to Sam after the divorce.

"Look, Em, I'm telling you what I saw. You can do what you want with the information."

"I'm sure it wasn't as bad as it looked. I know Richard wouldn't do that to me."

"Yeah, I knew Matt wouldn't either," she scoffed. "Sometimes, you're so naive."

"Naive?"

"Look at the facts, Em." She set her cup down and clasped her hands together. "He's out a lot, he's distracted, he's been spotted carrying

on with a beautiful woman at a fancy restaurant…" She paused to look her sister in the eye.

The list could have come straight out of the Cheater's Handbook. Emily met her gaze.

"Any changes in the bedroom?"

Emily hesitated. Their conversation felt more like an interrogation. She sighed and avoided eye contact. "He's been sleeping in the guest room for a couple weeks."

Samantha let the words hang in the air between them.

Emily set down her cup and studied her sister. Samantha built a pretty good case, but it was all circumstantial.

"I'm sorry, Em, but a girl's got to protect herself, you know?"

Emily didn't respond.

They talked for another fifteen minutes, but Emily's mind was no longer on their conversation. She'd fixed her attention on a single dirty little word, an accusation. Naive—not a word she'd use to describe herself. Did Samantha mean naive only in matters of the heart, or was it evident in other areas of her life, as well? Perhaps one's naiveté was a selective mechanism, allowing a person to believe only the things they wanted to believe and reject those too painful to consider.

"Hi, Em," Sam said like she was right on time.

The interruption jolted Emily back to the present. She studied Sam's smiling face before she drank the last of her cold coffee.

An awkward silence followed. Emily stood, grabbed her phone, and dropped it in her purse. "I need to go."

CHAPTER **NINE**

Michael closed the car door, hesitated, then leaned his head into the open passenger window.

"I don't know if I can do this."

"It's not like this is your first time." Angie rolled her eyes. "I'll pick you up in a couple hours."

The car window closed before Michael could respond. Arthur stood in front of the bookstore, holding the door open like a doorman. Michael grabbed Arthur's arm and pulled him aside.

"I needed you yesterday. Where were you?"

Arthur smiled. "Did you rub the lamp?"

"Very funny. We need to talk."

"I'm here now. What's on your mind?"

"I think Richard... I... had an affair."

"Emily thought the same thing."

Michael waited for him to add something more. When he didn't, "I need to know what kind of man I was. Memories are coming back."

"And?"

"I don't like what I'm seeing."

Arthur opened the door. "Your memories are of who you were then, not necessarily who you are now or can be."

A man in a suit inside the store looked at Michael and tapped his wrist. Michael nodded then turned to Arthur.

"I have to go." Michael pointed a finger at Arthur. "Don't leave town."

Michael sat at a table, flanked by stacks of his books, an unfamiliar position. A line of people waited for his signature. A life-size cut-out of Michael, book in hand, stood next to the table on his left. He'd studied the unique characteristics of the large signature scrawled across the image.

Open the cover, replicate the signature, close the cover, hand the book back, repeat. Don't forget to smile.

He glanced at the cut-out from time to time to make sure he got the signature right, but not nearly as often as he checked the clock on the wall. He reminded himself that he would have to get used to this kind of thing. Two hours couldn't go by fast enough.

Halfway through the event, a forty-something woman with emerald-green eyes stepped forward and set her copy of his book on the table. Michael, head down, opened the front cover.

"Who should I make it out to?"

"Emily."

Michael looked up. Emily smiled.

Another shift.

Richard sat alone on a bench in the campus quad, open book in his lap. A barefoot beauty, books in one hand and sandals dangling from the other, strolled along a nearby path. Richard watched her dark hair dance on her shoulders.

As if she could feel his stare, she turned. Her hair swung in slow motion across her face before it bounced back into place, revealing the greenest eyes he'd ever seen and a smile that rocked his world.

Back in the bookstore, that same smile had Michael reeling again.

Emily waited for him to sign her book. "Is something wrong?"

His cheeks burned. He shook his head, signed the book, and handed it back to her. His gaze followed her as she walked away.

"Excuse me," he said to the next person in line, then hurried after Emily. He noticed her near the front door, her book open. She looked up when Michael called her name.

"Hi. This is going to sound weird..."

"No weirder than this, I imagine." She read Michael's inscription. "Best wishes Emily. Love, Michael Riordan."

He swallowed hard. "I... I'm sorry. I can fix that." He reached for the book.

Emily pulled it back. "No way, Jose. This is a collector's item."

"Can we pretend that never happened?"

"No... no we can't," she said with a smirk.

Michael took a deep breath. "I didn't think so." After an awkward pause, he added, "I have this feeling we've met."

She glanced at the signature, then back to Michael. "It appears that way, doesn't it?"

"It's really you." Michael raked his hands back through his hair.

"I can't argue with that." Emily studied him curiously, then smiled. "To be honest, we have met." She held up his book and pointed to the publisher's mark on the spine. "I work for Pendulum."

Quick recovery. "Yeah... that must be it."

Another awkward pause descended between them until Emily pointed to the door. "I should probably..."

His mind raced. *Don't let her go.* "Can I buy you a cup of coffee?"

"I don't know, can you? You seem a little—"

"I think I can handle it."

Emily frowned. "Now?"

Michael turned to look at the growing line. He caught the eye of the store manager, who held up his hands. "Probably not a good idea."

Michael took Emily's book, pulled a pen from his pocket, and wrote his cell number under his name. "That should fetch a better price."

Emily said nothing. She looked like she just scratched a winning lottery ticket.

Michael smiled on the inside as he handed her the book. "Call me."

Back home, Michael sat by the pool and re-played the day's events in his mind. It had been by far the best day of his short tenure as Michael Riordan, so a celebration was in order. He strolled into the kitchen and opened the big fridge. He searched for some form of alcohol. Beer or wine, it didn't matter as long as it was cold. He imagined that, like everything else in Michael's castle, it would be top shelf.

After several minutes, he called off the search. He thought it strange that Angie, of all people, would let something like this happen on her watch. Perhaps it was time for Michael to take some initiative with his life. He closed the refrigerator door. No reason he couldn't make a beer run himself. He knew how to drive. He'd known his way around before the accident. Surely, it would come back to him once he got behind the wheel again.

He spotted a note from Angie on the counter and picked it up. *Went out with a friend. Stay put until I get back.* He reminded himself who the boss was in this relationship. He pulled out his wallet. Driver's license… check. Credit card… check. He set off to find the car keys.

CHAPTER **TEN**

With the top down, Michael cruised the streets of his neighborhood until he found a way out. He followed the signs into town, wind in his hair and a smile on his face. A wave of familiarity washed over him while he waited for the light at the corner of Kirkland and Montgomery. His smile slipped away.

The light turned green, and the car behind him honked its horn. Without a second thought, he turned left onto Kirkland. He pulled over in front of house number 36, an average home on an average street. He had all he could do to keep from pulling into the driveway, as if the car, or perhaps he himself, was on autopilot. He stared for a moment at the broken coach lamp and the shrubs that needed trimming. A chill descended as if a December breeze had blown up the back of his shirt. He'd lived there before.

Eventually, Michael turned the car off and stepped into the street, aware that this was a bad idea. He walked across the lawn and climbed the porch steps. A dog barked inside, and an invisible fist punched him in the stomach. This was *his* porch. The one he'd seen in his flashback. He opened the lid on the mailbox and peeked inside.

"Can I help you?" A neighbor called from her doorway. He closed the lid quickly and turned toward the voice. He recognized the face. Gail something or other, the self-appointed neighborhood watch.

Michael blinked a few times and cleared his throat. "I… I'm looking for someone," he replied.

"In the mailbox?"

"Richard Dunham." He folded his arms across his chest. "He's an old friend."

Her expression softened, and she stepped out onto her porch. "I'm sorry, but you won't find him there."

"I thought this might be his house."

"It is… I mean, was. He passed away about a month ago. Car accident."

Michael descended the steps. He walked across the small lawn to a chain link fence where he rested his hands.

"I'm sorry to hear that." *You have no idea how sorry,* he thought. "How is Emily doing?"

"Oh, she's fine. I mean, it was difficult in the beginning, but she's moving on."

"Fine, huh?"

"I don't think they were getting along very well at the end."

Another memory resurfaced. Gail and her big nose—always sticking it in other people's business. If you looked up the word *busybody* in the dictionary, you'd find her picture.

"What makes you say that?" he asked.

"She threw him out one night shortly before the accident." She pointed to the side of her house. "I watched the whole thing from that window."

Of course you did.

"If you ask me, I think he was seeing someone on the side." She shook her head and exhaled sharply. "Poor Emily."

Michael had just about enough of this. "I should get going. But here's a little piece of advice…" He straightened up and wagged a finger in her direction. "Try keeping your nose in your own business and your opinions to yourself. You'll live longer."

"Well!" she said with a huff, then spun on her heel. The front door slammed, and she disappeared inside the house.

Michael smiled. She had that coming, he thought. What bothered him was that she might have been right. He drove off thinking that Emily appeared to have put his death behind her a little too quickly. He needed to know what happened between them. Had he betrayed her with another woman? That would be a capital offense, the mere suspicion of which was often enough to destroy a relationship. He needed to break the cycle, as Arthur had put it, but was it too late?

He reminded himself that until his run-in with his old neighbor, he'd been having a good day. No, a great day. He'd made an unexpected connection with Emily that was worthy of a scene in a movie—the awkward first meeting where the guy usually says or does something stupid, and the girl thinks it's charming but plays hard to get. In the end, the guy always manages to get the girl. Of course he wasn't naive enough to think that nothing could go wrong, but Act 1 seemed to follow the script.

Seeing the old house reminded him of the nights spent grilling steaks on the deck out back. If grilling was an art form, then Richard was Picasso. Each week he would produce another masterpiece, properly seasoned and cooked to perfection. Over the past ten years, Saturday night steak dinners had become something of a tradition at the Dunham house.

Tonight, he would treat Angela to a juicy porterhouse. He'd taken out his frustrations on her the past few days and hoped he might make it up to her with a nice dinner. On a more personal note, his meeting with Emily that morning was surely cause for celebration.

In the checkout line at the market, he thought of how he might teach Michael the proper way to grill a piece of beef. The absurdity of that thought caused him to laugh aloud in the grocery store. Embarrassed, he explained to the cashier that it was an inside joke, which only made him laugh more.

He stopped at a liquor store and bought a bottle of Merlot to have with dinner, a bottle of Pinot, and a six-pack to have, well, whenever he felt like it. Pinot Noir was Emily's favorite. Some reviewers described it as the most romantic of wines, and Emily sometimes referred to it by its nickname—sex in a glass. He planned to share that bottle with her.

Michael whistled a tune as he pulled the bottles of wine from a bag and set them on the kitchen counter. He deposited the Pinot, the beer, and the steaks in the fridge.

"Hello?" Angie's voice drifted in from another room.

"In here."

"Got anything to eat?"

"I'm sure we can find—"

"Have you lost your mind?" Angie stood in the doorway, the color gone from her face. She stared at the wine bottle.

Michael shrugged. "That's what they tell me."

"This isn't funny, Michael." She took a few steps toward him and stabbed a finger in his face. "You're an alcoholic!"

CHAPTER **ELEVEN**

Michael stared at the finger pointed in his face while Angie waited for a response. His mind took him back to another time and place when he stared at the business end of an accusing finger.

He stood in someone's kitchen. Red, white, and blue streamers and the sound of a party outside. Gunfire, no… fireworks, echoed in the distance. Emily's sister, Samantha, never afraid to speak her mind, was attached to the other end of the finger.

"I know what you're up to… Dick!"

Samantha folded her arms across her chest. Her back stiffened and she stood a little taller. "You'd better stop sneaking around and tell her."

Richard frowned. "Tell who what?"

"I don't like people lying to my little sister. I'm funny that way." The finger was back. "If you don't tell her, I will."

Angie waved her hand in front of Michael's face. "Are you listening to me?"

Michael returned to the present. "What?"

"I said you're an alcoholic."

Michael shook his head. "Nooo… that's not possible. You must be mistaken."

"Mistaken?" Angie's hands returned to her hips. "Do you hear yourself?"

He raked his hands through his hair. "This just keeps getting better and better." He didn't need any more setbacks. Arthur would hear about this.

Angie took Michael's right hand and placed a sobriety coin in his palm. He turned it slowly in his fingers.

"You have one just like it," she said in a fragile voice. "It's like I don't even know you anymore."

"Michael handed the coin back. "You don't understand. Things are different now."

"Really? How?"

He wanted to tell her, but he couldn't find the right words.

Angie flashed a skeptical look, then shrugged. "You're probably right." She picked up the bottle and carried it to the counter.

Michael relaxed. "There's glasses in the—"

"I know where the glasses are."

Angie shattered the neck of the bottle against the sink. Michael protested as he watched the wine disappear into the drain. Tears slid down Angie's cheeks when she turned around.

Michael exhaled sharply, then pulled her in for a hug. "I'm sorry. I really didn't know."

She buried her head in his chest. "You big dope," she whispered.

Michael and his sister talked at the kitchen table for the next hour. Angie described their strained relationship during Michael's *dark* period after his wife died. She admitted that she'd been no stranger to depression after her divorce. The two found common ground—alcohol addiction—in the aftermath. Eventually, they checked into the same rehab facility to face their demons together.

Michael's story caused him some concern. He silently wondered if the problem would continue given his new circumstances. He decided to proceed with caution.

Angie displayed a great deal of compassion for her older brother. Michael recognized why they'd been close. He'd grown fond of her in the short time he'd known her. She could be snarky, but he had to take some, well most, of the responsibility for that. He'd taken his frustrations out on her undeservedly.

Fortunately, their conversation took a turn for the better, and they reminisced about happier times. Well, Angie reminisced. Michael learned a great deal about the man whose shoes—and life—he'd stepped into.

Before Angie left, she offered to help him locate his coin. He promised to look for it himself, but she insisted. They eventually found it, and he set it on the desk in his study.

"No, Michael. It doesn't work that way." She picked up the coin and handed it to him. "You need to carry it with you."

"I plan to spend a lot of time in here."

"I don't care. You need to keep it with you wherever you go."

"I'm not going anywhere right now."

Her back stiffened and she looked at him with insistent eyes. "You need to go to a meeting."

He wondered if they'd had this conversation before. He gently squeezed her shoulder. "I'll think about it. I just need some time to—"

"You don't have that kind of time. You never will."

Those were Michael's demons, not his, but she wouldn't understand. He didn't need any tokens. He couldn't risk anything that might arouse Emily's suspicion—or worse, scare her away.

Michael paced around the kitchen after Angie left. The image of Samantha's accusing finger returned and refused to leave him alone. What did she know? He needed to find out. He sat at the kitchen table and rested his head on folded arms. He closed his eyes, and it was the Fourth of July.

Dozens of people milled about in a sprawling backyard. Many of the adults clustered in the shade of two large Japanese Maple trees, while others hovered around the drinks table on the veranda. Children waited in line near the ten-foot slide, situated at one end of the kidney-shaped pool. Those already in the water laughed and squealed.

Richard picked up a beer and wandered over to a large gas grill, and watched the man he now recognized as Emily's oldest brother Frank, flip a row of burgers.

Frank glanced up. "What's the matter? You don't look like you're having fun."

"No, no. This is great, Frank. I just have a lot on my mind."

Richard and Frank had bonded over a common interest—classic cars. Particularly, the restoration of late 60s and early 70s muscle cars. Frank had recently completed the restoration of a 1969 Dodge Charger, the car popularized in the Dukes of Hazard television series. The two men helped each other out when a job required more than two hands.

"How's the Blue Knight running?"

"She's out of commission until I replace the timing chain. I might try to work on her after the party."

"There's a big auction in Jersey this weekend. Maybe you'd like to tag along."

Richard shrugged. "I'd love to, but I'm not sure I can get away for the whole weekend."

Emily's older brother, Tommy, strolled up the driveway dressed in his police uniform. Muscular frame, square jaw, and intense eyes like a shark—the kind of guy you go out of your way to stay out of his.

Frank set a spatula down and picked up a bottle of beer. "That sonofabitch Tommy will be late for his own funeral."

"Has he been staying out of trouble?"

Frank snorted. "No more than usual."

Richard stole a glance at Emily while Frank turned the sausages.

"How about we make it a day trip?" Frank moved a couple steaks away from a burst of flame. "We'll take my plane. I can have us there in an hour. Less with a good tail wind."

Richard watched Emily. "That might work."

Frank loaded the meat onto two huge platters. "Let's go feed the masses," he said.

When he'd finished eating, Richard sat in the shade of one of the big market umbrellas and scanned the festivities. Emily and Tommy talked with their sister by the pool. Samantha wore cut-off shorts and an Aerosmith t-shirt. She'd tied her auburn hair in a ponytail and pulled it through the back of a baseball cap.

Richard waved when she looked in his direction. Samantha did not reciprocate. He watched her talk with Tommy for a few minutes before she turned and headed toward the house.

"Hey, Sam," he said as she walked past.

She glared and continued on her way.

Michael raised his head quickly as if someone had caught him asleep on the job. His eyes darted around his kitchen. He remembered something. The secret he'd been hiding, the one he'd assumed Samantha had threatened to expose. He hadn't slept with Carolyn, after all. He'd remember something like that. Perhaps he wasn't such a royal douchebag. Perhaps he was just your run-of-the-mill douchebag. The kind that would let a beautiful woman convince him to invest his life savings on a bad stock tip.

CHAPTER **TWELVE**

Emily pulled the cork from a bottle of Pinot Noir, poured a generous glass, then leaned back against her kitchen counter. It had been a difficult day at work, and she needed to unwind. She picked up the bottle and headed for the living room. A picture of her and Richard sat on the piano, and she turned it face down before she continued on to the sofa. Halfway through her second glass of wine, the hard edges of her frustration softened, and she suddenly had the urge to play the piano.

She set her glass down next to the overturned picture and sat on the bench. She'd struggled with the timing of Richard's death, unable to confront him with the evidence that Sam had provided. After a brief period of mourning, her attempts to move on often felt like two steps forward and one step back.

When she played, her cares melted and drifted away on the sweet sounds that filled the room. She thumbed through her music, and picked up an old Carole King song book, a gift from Richard. The songs had been favorites back in college, but now she had difficulty finding one whose words didn't feel like a knife in her heart. Songs like *It's Too Late, So Far Away,* and *Will You Love Me Tomorrow* made her feel worse.

While the lyrics seemed to bring only pain, the songs themselves invoked memories of happier times—meeting Richard, falling in love, and starting a family. She focused on these feelings as she played. They lasted for a song or two, but as her memory moved closer to the present, the facade crumbled.

She remembered feeling like she was slipping down on his list of priorities. The last time she asked him if he still loved her, his answer had been less than convincing.

They walked in the park together, an outing that Emily had proposed so they might spend some much-needed time together. Richard, of course, was too busy at first, but Emily persisted. She suggested Franklin Park, a favorite spot of theirs.

Franklin Park, situated within the city limits, encompassed approximately sixty acres of woodlands and recreation areas. Richard and Emily walked together along the trail that encircled a large pond near the center of the park. The stone fountain in the middle of the pond sprayed water into the air in every direction, and provided a picturesque backdrop.

Emily glanced up at the Overlook, an observation platform built into a large rock formation at the north end of the pond. Countless relationships had started or ended there. Lovers visited day and night, stealing a kiss or a tender moment in each other's arms, or just watching the lighted fountain churn up the water some twenty feet below.

Richard and Emily were no exception. She remembered their first kiss, and the day she'd brought him there to announce her pregnancy. Over the years, it had become a landmark in their lives together.

The mood was light and even playful at first.

"Do you remember the first time you brought me here?" Emily asked.

"Hmmm..." Richard scratched above his lip to conceal a smile. "Can't say that I do."

She lifted an eyebrow. "Oh, really?"

"Well... I've brought so many women here over the years, you can't seriously expect me to remember—"

"Yeah, right." She punched his shoulder. "You were such a nerd."

"I asked you, didn't I?"

"You did. I must say I was pleasantly surprised."

Neither said anything for a moment.

"You don't regret it do you?" she asked.

"I didn't... until you broke my heart."

"I'm sorry for that, but it made you fight for me. It was romantic." She hooked her arm in his. "Whatever happened to my romantic warrior?"

They turned onto the narrow path that led to the Overlook platform. Emily leaned against the railing and looked out over the pond. Richard stood next to her in silence.

"Do you still love me, Richard?"

He hesitated. "Yes... of course. Of course I do."

"I want to hear you say it like you mean it."

Before he could respond, his phone rang, and he reached for it instinctively. Emily folded her arms across her chest. He glanced at the screen then sent the call to voicemail. He looked up. "I'm sorry."

She rolled her eyes. "Give me that thing so I can throw it in the pond."

Richard slipped his phone back into his pocket.

Emily sighed and rested her arms on the railing. "Are you afraid to die?" she asked after an awkward silence.

"Why... why would you ask that?"

"No reason." Emily turned to him. "It's just that we're not getting any younger."

"It's a little early to talk about dying, don't you think?"

"Perhaps." She looked back out over the water. "I started a bucket list."

"You're not sick, are you?"

"Would it matter?"

Richard shot her a sideways glare before turning away.

Emily grabbed his arm. "I'm sorry. That was mean. I'm not dying or anything like that."

Richard said nothing.

She raised her eyebrows playfully. "Want to know what's number one on the list?"

"Only if it doesn't involve a butcher knife and the family jewels."

"I said I was sorry." She paused. "I want to go to Ireland."

"Really?"

"Grandma McKenna used to tell me stories about growing up near Dublin. I want to walk the streets she walked. Connect with her spirit."

"I knew you two were close, but her spirit?" Richard shook his head. "Maybe we can just get one of those Ouija boards and—"

"I'm serious, Richard. I need this. We need this."

"You want me to go with you?"

"Of course." Disappointment washed over her face momentarily. "You wouldn't want me wandering around chasing ghosts all by myself, would you?"

"No. I guess not, but we don't have to do it right away, we could—"

"I want to go soon."

Richard swallowed hard. "Define soon."

"We could go in the fall," she said.

"THIS fall?" He cleared his throat. "What about the kitchen? We can't do both. You said—"

"I have to do this."

"I'm not sure I can get away," Richard said just before his phone rang.

She shook her head and whispered, "Sometimes I don't know why I bother."

Emily stopped playing the piano. The good memories, like Richard, slowly faded before they vanished altogether, leaving her sad and alone. She took another drink of wine and decided then and there to sell the damn piano.

CHAPTER **THIRTEEN**

Emily lay in bed with another glass of wine. The bedside lamp burned a little too brightly, and she reached for the dimmer switch. Michael Riordan's book sat next to a pair of reading glasses on the nightstand. She picked it up and opened the cover. A curious smile crossed her lips when she read his inscription again. *What was that about?* She played back their conversation, thinking he sounded more like a nervous teenager than a successful adult author.

The book had been interesting, the story of a promising young athlete whose dreams had been dashed by an injury in college. He went into a tailspin and became addicted to pain medication and alcohol. The woman he eventually married helped him get clean and stay that way. At her suggestion, he took a job working with children at a state-run facility and found his purpose. He returned to school and earned a degree in social work. After twenty-one years of marriage, a boating accident that killed his wife sent him to the brink again.

It read more like a memoir than a novel, and she wondered how much of it came from real life experience. She wanted to know more. She ran the tip of her finger slowly over the phone number he'd added to his signature. She had nothing to lose at this point.

She'd done her best to push away the memories that had resurfaced earlier that evening, but more bubbled up. She took another sip of wine as scenes from Richard's memorial service played in her mind like a bad movie.

Emily stood with Lexi alongside the open casket in one of the Victorian-style sitting rooms at the Grossman Funeral Home. Flowers spilled from dozens of vases crowded on the polished mahogany side tables.

Lexi had spent the previous night gathering photos of her father from scrapbooks and old shoe boxes and had assembled the visual remembrance that rested on a large easel near the entrance to the room. A gilded guest book sat on a pedestal just inside the door to record the names of those who came to offer their sympathy and bid final farewell.

Some of their closest friends and family arrived first and receiving them had proved more difficult than she'd imagined. Only a handful knew of their situation, but this was neither the time nor the place for such conversation. She stole a glance at the casket from the corner of her eye. Richard wore his favorite charcoal gray suit and red tie.

After a difficult first hour listening to how sorry everyone was for her loss, she stood with a wad of tissues in her hand, grateful for her decision not to wear mascara. The line slowed for a moment and Samantha approached. She stood in front of Emily, their faces almost touching.

"She's here," Samantha whispered, her eyes wide.

"Who's here?"

"The woman from the restaurant."

Emily peeked around Samantha.

"Don't look now," Sam scolded.

Emily straightened. "Which one is she?"

Samantha gave a slight turn of her head and a sideways glance. "Over there. By the photos. Dark hair, little black dress, you can't miss her. She's the best-looking woman in the room... present company excluded, of course."

Emily peeked again. A tall woman, dressed for a night out on the town, stood near the easel. A black designer dress did an admirable job of showcasing her long, slender legs.

"You've got to be kidding," Emily said. "She's the one you saw him with at the restaurant?" She twisted the ring on her finger.

"I'm afraid so, Em."

The line backed up, so Emily motioned for Sam to move on.

Emily kept a close eye on the woman in the little black dress. At least Richard had good taste. The thought offered little consolation, and she cried. No one noticed.

The woman knelt in front of the casket and lingered a little longer than most. She stood and flipped her long brown hair over her shoulder. Emily thought she saw a tear.

The little black dress approached, and Emily's heart beat double time. Her face burned and her ears pounded so loud she feared she'd be unable to hear anything the woman had to say. Perhaps she didn't want to.

The woman stopped directly in front of her. "I'm sorry for your loss."

If she tries to hug me, I swear I'm going to punch her in the face, Emily thought. She took a moment to regain her composure before she reluctantly took the woman's hand. "Thank you… uh…"

"My name is Carolyn Giordano. I was a client of Richard's. He was a good man."

Emily nodded, struggling to hide her contempt.

Carolyn turned to leave, then stopped. She flipped her damn hair again and looked back. "I own a restaurant here in town. Please come by sometime." she smiled. "It's Adrianna's on Third Avenue. Bring your family. Dinner is on me."

Emily forced a smile. "Thank you."

She exhaled sharply as she watched Carolyn walk away. The tears returned. Again, no one noticed.

A week later she found the smoking gun inside the envelope of Richard's personal effects that had sat unopened on the dining room table. She stared at the contents that she'd spilled onto the table— Richard's wallet, cell phone, wedding ring, and sixty-five cents in change. She touched each item, moving them a little as if they were slightly out of place.

She picked up Richard's cell phone and turned it on. A picture of the two of them from their first cruise together appeared on the screen. It reminded her of one of the best times in her life. Holding back tears, she scrolled through his contacts list. Many unfamiliar names rolled past; business associates, she assumed. Her heart stopped at Carolyn's name. She didn't want to believe it meant anything more than the others.

Unsure of what to do with his stuff, she picked up the envelope to return its contents. Something else remained inside—a folded piece of paper. She reached in and grasped the edge of the paper firmly between her thumb and forefinger. An uneasy feeling started in the pit of her stomach and spread outward in waves. She set the envelope down and hesitated before she unfolded the paper—a letter.

A chill descended on her when she read the salutation: Dear Emily. She checked the signature—Carolyn Giordano. The little black dress. She read the contents of the letter. Her pulse quickened, and her stomach twisted. She finished reading, set it on the table, and wiped her eyes. Her attempt to read it again was met with a wall of tears. She shook her head in disbelief. This was it, she thought. The proof she hoped she would never find.

Back in her bedroom, Emily closed Michael's book and slid it onto the nightstand. She finished the rest of the wine and set her empty glass on top of the book. She had a phone call to make in the morning.

CHAPTER **FOURTEEN**

Michael sat on a bench in Franklin Park, notebook in his lap and pen in hand. He wrote down more memories while he waited for Emily. He remembered the first day he'd met Emily in college.

Two beds, a couple of small desks, and a dorm-sized refrigerator on the floor cluttered the small room. Richard's college roommate, Tony, sat on the edge of his bed, hands clasped and elbows on his knees.

"You've got to help me out," he said. "I thought roommates had each other's backs?"

"Forget it. No more blind dates."

"C'mon, man, I need you," he whined. "This sophomore's a tough nut to crack. She won't go anywhere with me unless we bring our roommates."

"Smart girl. Have you met the roommate?"

"Don't worry. You're gonna love her."

Tony could sell ice to an Eskimo, and they eventually struck a deal. They agreed to meet for drinks Friday night.

Bodies packed the campus pub, and Richard swam through the crowd, hoping Tony had been there early enough to get a table. He noticed his friend at the back of the room. Tony motioned toward an empty seat as Richard approached.

Two women sat at the table with him. Richard's stomach flipped. "It's her!"

It'd been little more than a whisper, insignificant in the noisy bar, but the green-eyed girl from the quad turned in his direction the second the words left his mouth. Their eyes met. He held her gaze, and for a moment, they were alone in the room. Slowly, other people reappeared, and Richard wiped his palms on his jeans.

Tony stood. "Hey buddy, glad you made it." He mouthed the words thank you.

Richard's gaze never left the brunette on his left.

Tony sat between the two girls and gestured toward the blonde on his right, who looked bored. He winked. "This is Charlotte Johnson."

Richard nodded and forced a smile. The roommate. Evidently, his green-eyed mystery girl was the tough nut.

"And this," Tony gestured to his left, "is Emily McKenna."

At least now she had a name.

After a week, Tony gave up and moved on. It took Richard another week to work up the nerve to ask her out. She said yes, and they had a burger and a stroll through Franklin Park at sunset.

He shook his head to clear it. His life had begun that day, then ended abruptly, but it appears he'd been given a second chance. He had a singular focus now, but there were many unanswered questions.

Would Emily feel some strange feeling like déjà vu when they spend time together? Was there some sort of energy signature souls gave off that could be detected and recognized subconsciously by others? He wondered if she'd felt anything when they met in the bookstore. Would he be able to keep his secret, or would he spill his guts immediately? He had no similar experience to call upon.

He checked the time on his phone. He recalled silly little details about her—the way her green eyes sparkled when she got excited, the way she laughed at his jokes even when they weren't funny, the way she twirled her hair around her finger when she was nervous. He continued to write down every detail.

A dog barked. Michael looked up. "Bogey?"

A Yellow Labrador Retriever ran toward him with Emily in hot pursuit. Bogey stood on the bench with his front paws and licked Michael's face.

"Hey, Bogey. How's my boy?" he said without thinking.

Emily stopped and stared at the two of them.

"I'm sorry," he said as he stood up.

"What did you call him?"

"Uh… boy, I called him boy." Michael shifted his weight. "He's a male, right?"

Emily eyed him suspiciously. "He's never done anything like that before."

Michael scratched Bogey behind the ears. "No worries. I'm fine."

"He's usually well behaved around strangers."

Michael smiled.

"He ran to you like you were old friends."

"Uh... yeah, that was a little strange, wasn't it?"

Michael picked up the end of Bogey's leash and handed it to Emily. "Reminds me of a dog I once had."

"His name is Bogart," she said. "We've always called him Bogey."

He smiled. "Casablanca was my favorite movie."

Emily studied him for a moment through squinted eyes. "I like that one, too."

They headed off down the trail. A jogger with an iPod strapped to her arm passed them.

"I'm glad you called," Michael said after they'd walked in silence for a few moments.

"When a famous author leaves his book signing to chase after you..."

Michael smiled. "You bring along a dog for protection."

Emily shrugged. "Yeah... that didn't exactly work the way I planned." She pointed at his notebook. "Working on another book?"

"Uh... sort of." He tucked the notebook out of sight.

"Don't worry. Your secret's safe with me."

"Oh yeah, you work for my publisher. How did you end up there?"

"I worked for a smaller publisher for years. I decided to change jobs after my husband died. Same position, more money."

Bogey stopped to sniff something in the grass. Emily slowed. "So, what's the next book about?"

Michael hesitated. "I could tell you, but then I'd have to kill you."

Bogey moved on and they resumed their pace.

"That wouldn't be wise," she warned. "I went on a couple dates with ADA Phillip Morgan. I think he's sweet on me."

Michael stopped in his tracks. Emily took a few more steps before noticing. She turned to Michael. "What? You weren't really planning to kill me... were you?"

"A couple dates?" He frowned. "Are you two...?"

She cocked her head. "Would that be a problem?"

You bet it would! "No... no." He caught up to her. "Of course not."

"It's nothing serious at this point. I met him at a fundraiser and he asked me out. I refused at first, but he was persistent. Evidently, he's used to getting what he wants."

"And that doesn't concern you a little?"

"Well, maybe a little, but he's friends with my brother Tommy."

"A lawyer, huh?"

She twirled a few strands of hair around her finger.

"It was so cold last winter," Michael said to break the awkward silence, "that I saw a lawyer with his hands in his *own* pockets."

"Michael! That's not nice." She gently slapped his shoulder. "You don't know anything about him." Their eyes met, and she studied him.

"I'm sorry. I just don't want to see you get hurt."

"So, you think lawyers are incapable of having an honest relationship?"

"Your husband died in a car accident six weeks ago."

"So, what's your point?"

"Isn't that a little soon to be..."

"I don't owe Richard anything."

A man wearing sunglasses and a Red Sox cap watched them from a park bench as they passed.

"That was creepy," Emily said.

"I think I saw him at the book signing."

They walked in silence for a few moments.

Michael cleared his throat. "How serious is this thing with Phillip?"

"Depends on who you ask."

CHAPTER **FIFTEEN**

Michael arrived at Rhonda's office a little early and was greeted with a big smile and an even bigger hug.

"How's my favorite writer?" she said when she finally released him. He sat in one of the two chairs that faced her desk—a big desk, a power desk. He expected nothing less. A framed poster on the wall showed a hang glider stepping off a cliff above the words 'You only live once.' He smiled and shook his head.

"If you're talking about me, I'm doing as well as can be expected, I guess." Michael shifted uncomfortably in his chair. They exchanged small talk for a few minutes.

"Okay, Michael, enough foreplay. Let's get down to business."

"I don't think I've ever heard a woman say that before."

"Tell me you're almost done with the next book."

Michael shrugged apologetically.

"Okay, but you've started it. What's it about?"

"Did I mention that I drive a sweet little Beamer? You can probably see it from your window."

"Michael, I've seen your car. You need to get serious. They want a manuscript yesterday."

He adjusted his collar. "What if I don't have another one in me?"

"Then I'd say we should have had this conversation before you signed a two-book deal."

"My situation's changed."

"Unfortunately, the terms of your contract haven't."

Technically, *he* hadn't signed any contracts. Surely, no legal precedents for such a situation existed.

"What about the accident?" He had to find some other way out. "Maybe I can get an extension or something."

"Been there, done that." Rhonda's eyes narrowed. "I don't want to play that card too many times."

"Why not?"

"We could all be in a lot of trouble if the truth gets out."

"The truth?"

"Oh yeah, that's right." Rhonda waved a hand in mock dismissal. "You were so drunk you couldn't possibly have remembered." She shifted to a more defensive tone. "Beside the fact that you almost killed me, you put me in a difficult position. If I let you take the rap, you'd be—"

Michael straightened in his chair. "You were in the car?"

"Lucky for you, I told them I was driving. I had to bend over backwards to keep your name out of it."

Michael closed his eyes and shook his head while Rhonda walked around the desk and sat next to him.

"It wasn't your first offense." Her voice softened. "You would have gone to jail... and lost your book deal."

"How did you make it go away?"

"I had a friend in the DA's office."

Michael's throat tightened, and he swallowed hard. "A man named Richard Dunham died."

"And nothing we do will bring him back."

"How much did it cost?"

Rhonda stood. "Like I said, I had to bend over backwards." She returned to her seat behind the desk. "I might be able to hold the publisher off for another week or two."

Michael moved his lips, but no sound emerged. He needed some air. He stood and walked toward the door.

"Michael," Rhonda called.

Michael hesitated as he reached for the doorknob.

"Just get me some pages. ASAP."

He nodded, then let himself out.

Michael drove by Emily's house on the way home. A kitchen supply delivery truck had backed up to the garage door. Two contractor's pickups were parked in the street. The project that he and Emily had planned for years was moving forward without him, most likely financed with his life insurance money. He wrestled with the thought that he'd meant more to her dead than alive.

They had been saving for the renovation for a while, and had accumulated nearly enough to get started, but Emily threw a monkey wrench into their plans with the Ireland trip. Then along came Carolyn. Admittedly, he'd been attracted to her, and perhaps had given her more attention than his other clients, but he still believed that they hadn't done anything inappropriate. However, Carolyn offered a way out of his financial dilemma—a once in a lifetime investment. A virtual sure thing. Until it wasn't. He'd invested their savings, then doubled down with a loan against their home. A foolish mistake in hindsight, one that may have ultimately caused his demise.

Emily would surely stay with Lexi until the kitchen renovation was complete. If he could only remember where she lived. Michael squeezed the wheel amid his mounting frustration. He drove his fancy car down one suburban, middle-class street after another, some vaguely familiar, others not so much.

He had money now, but it was too late. It wouldn't help him get his family back. It wouldn't even help him get his memory back. Perhaps it's about something more than just money.

Michael never noticed the stop sign on the corner of the busy intersection. Another driver laid on his horn and swerved to avoid Michael's car. The near miss brought Michael back from his reverie. He pulled over when he reached the other side of the intersection, muscles tense and knuckles white on the wheel.

A familiar feeling of terror washed over him, and brought him back to that dark, rain-soaked night.

He'd been in a hurry to get home to tell Emily the truth about what he'd done. He hoped to head off the lies that Carolyn planned to use to derail his marriage. It was blackmail, but the circumstantial evidence would be hard to ignore at a time when his relationship with Emily had hit a new low. All it needed was a bit of false testimony from someone like Carolyn to secure an indictment.

Richard sped south on Route 7. The wind picked up, and a wall of low dark clouds swirled before him in the half-light. He pressed the speaker button on his cell phone and speed-dialed Emily's number. No answer.

Rain burst from the sky and the wet pavement swallowed up his headlights. If he'd been honest in the first place, none of this would be happening. He rehearsed what he would say and wondered how Emily might receive it. Would she believe him or Carolyn? Carolyn was a master of persuasion.

A stop sign flashed past his window. He hit the brakes hard. Light suddenly flooded the car from the passenger window. The impact sounded like a shotgun blast, and his stomach twisted. Time unfolded in slow motion. Tiny diamonds of glass sprayed inward, sparkling in the light as they raced across his vision only inches in front of his eyes. Metal scraped against metal with a gut-wrenching sound, and the car flipped sideways.

For a moment, up was down and down was up. The seatbelt bit into his chest and air escaped his lungs like a deflating balloon. The car turned over three more times before it stopped against a large oak tree.

Richard blinked, barely conscious, but grateful for the stillness. Only the slow spinning of one of the wheels broke the silence.

Arthur's voice echoed in his head. "It's pretty arrogant to believe we always have tomorrow."

He tried to move, but he was trapped. The side of his head felt like he'd been hit with a sledgehammer. Blackness engulfed his vision. It started at the edges and advanced inward until it filled his sight and swallowed him whole.

CHAPTER **SIXTEEN**

Michael flipped through the pages of his notebook. He opened a desk drawer, pulled out the photo of Richard and Emily, and propped it up next to his laptop. His fingers tapped out CHAPTER ONE, and he stared at the screen.

Memories had flowed freely for the past several days, like a frozen river after a January thaw. Gaps still existed in his memory, which he assumed would be filled-in over time. However, he had an uneasy feeling that he hadn't known Emily as well as he should have.

Had he simply been going through the motions? No. He refused to believe that. He fought for her when she ended it in college. He'd won her back, married her, and spent twenty-three years with her. The uneasy feeling returned. He could have paid more attention. He hadn't had a clue what was at the top of her bucket list. He didn't even know she had one.

Angie appeared in the doorway. She folded her arms and leaned against the frame. "What's for dinner?"

"Uh..." Michael closed his laptop. "I hadn't thought about it."

"What are you working on?"

Michael shifted uncomfortably in his chair while Angie waited for an answer. He turned to face her. "Why don't you take a turn in the kitchen?"

"Szechuan Palace, it is." She brushed her palms together. "You want the usual?"

"The usual?"

"Yeah. Typical, customary, habitually occurring. C'mon Michael, you're a writer."

Emily loved Chinese food and they'd ordered take-out often. Szechuan Palace had been one of their favorites. Michael stared, lost in another memory.

Wine glasses and open Chinese food containers sat on the coffee table. Richard and Emily laughed and talked in hushed tones on the floor in front of the sofa. They watched the New Year's ball drop on television while Lexi slept in her pajamas behind them.

They counted down the last ten seconds in unison. The number 2000 flashed on the screen. A long kiss followed their Happy New Year wishes. They kissed again and slid down onto the floor.

Lexi opened her eyes and peeked over the edge of the sofa cushion. "Mommy and Daddy... are you okay?"

Richard and Emily laughed a secret laugh. They grabbed her and pulled her to the floor for a group hug.

Angie placed her hands on her hips. "Well?"

Michael nodded, annoyed at the interruption. "I'm sure that'll be fine."

He rested his elbows on his closed laptop as she walked away.

Michael sat across the kitchen table from Angie. They ate in silence. He watched her manipulate a pair of chopsticks like a pro.

He cleared his throat before he spoke. "I realize that lately I've been a little..."

"Cranky?"

"I was going to say preoccupied."

"You say tomato..."

"I'm sorry."

"Obviously something is bothering you. Did you ever think that maybe I can help?"

"I doubt it."

Angie's eyes held equal parts of fear and disappointment. "It's you and me against the world, remember? We've been through hell together. No secrets."

Michael pushed the food around on his plate.

"OK. Maybe I've been a little cranky, myself. I'm scared, Michael. You haven't been the same since the accident." She paused. "I just want things to go back to the way they were."

"That makes two of us."

After an awkward silence, Michael changed the subject. "Do you know a Phillip Morgan?"

She raised an eyebrow. "*A* Phillip Morgan? I think you mean *the* Phillip Morgan. Who doesn't know him?" She frowned above a curious smile. "Why?"

"Uh… no reason."

"He's hot! He's gotta be the most eligible bachelor on the planet."

Thanks, Ang. That's what I needed to hear.

She pointed her chopsticks in his direction. "You're not gay, are you?"

"What?"

"A switch-hitter, maybe?"

"Stop it." He stood. "Forget I asked." Michael left the room.

"Your turn to clean up," she called after him.

Michael returned to his office and closed the door. He opened his laptop and typed Phillip Morgan's name into the search box. The first of nearly eighteen-thousand pages displayed in less than a second. *Okay, so he's popular.* He wondered how many hits Michael Riordan's name would produce. Perhaps he'd try that later. Right now, he needed to know everything there was to know about *the* Phillip Morgan.

Phillip Morgan had been born into a prominent Springfield family, and grew up knowing the benefits of privilege. Even at an early age, he was no stranger to the limelight. He excelled at everything, including good looks. His father, the Honorable Bartholomew Morgan, opened all the right doors, grooming him to take his seat on the bench someday.

Presently the Assistant District Attorney for the City of Springfield, Phillip was something of a local hero and the popular choice for DA in the upcoming election. It was all part of the plan—stepping stones to the Governor's office. It appeared that Phillip had all the right cards and has been playing them as he'd been taught.

Michael skimmed several more pages of stories and press releases, most singing praises, but a small percentage appeared to suggest a shadow side, and a need to expose it before Phillip's rising star could reach the higher echelons of the state's political machine.

Clearly, *the* Phillip Morgan would do whatever it took to get what he wanted.

CHAPTER **SEVENTEEN**

Emily had never been to the bar in the front of *Autour du Monde*, let alone seated for dinner. Phillip, on the other hand, knew the maître d' and was accustomed to getting the best table in the house, even on short notice. Heads turned and people whispered when he entered a room. He held Emily's chair, and she sat.

The sommelier looked on while Phillip swirled and tasted the wine then nodded his approval.

Phillip raised his glass. "To fine wine and beautiful company."

Emily touched her glass to his, then brought it to her lips. If the food was as good as the wine, she was in for a treat. The view across the table wasn't too bad, either.

Phillip had a classic Mediterranean look, presumably from his mother's side of the family. His closely cropped black hair provided a striking contrast with hazel eyes that appeared more gray than brown. He wore a custom-tailored suit that hung flawlessly from his broad shoulders, and she guessed that his shirt cost more than her entire ensemble.

Looking across the table at Phillip Morgan in *Autour du Monde* felt like a dream—the glamour of being with someone rich and powerful who could give her everything she wanted. Emily got caught up in it. Part of her screamed for a reality check, while another part of her—the part that was in control at the moment—told her to enjoy the ride. After all, how often does an opportunity like this come along?

The beef bourguignon was to die for. After their flaming desserts had been extinguished and consumed, Phillip ordered another drink. Emily studied him as he spoke to the waiter. While she missed Richard's sense of humor, Phillip's sense of style and knowledge of everyone and everything in Springfield impressed her. But what impressed her most was that he deliberately left his cell phone in the car. Little things like that could win a girl's heart.

Phillip, with his designer suit and heir-apparent attitude, ushered Emily past the doorman and into the night air. He slipped the man a folded bill, and Emily took hold of his arm.

"The food was fabulous," she said, then stumbled on the first step.

Phillip caught her. "It appears you enjoyed the wine a little too much."

"I imagine that bottle cost more than my car," she said when she recovered her balance. "I wasn't going to waste any."

"I happen to think you're worth it."

The valet approached, but Phillip waved him off. "Let's take a walk. It's a beautiful night, and Armory Square is only a few blocks away."

At the heart of the recent downtown renaissance, Armory Square boasted a collection of upscale shops, eateries, and night clubs. Phillip informed the valet that they would return shortly, and they headed off in that direction.

The two walked silently for almost a block. Emily noticed Phillip glance at her every few seconds.

"What's on your mind?" she asked, her eyes on the sidewalk.

"There's something that's been troubling me."

"Don't be shy, Phillip. Tell me what it is."

"I've been informed that you've been spending time with another man in Franklin Park."

"His name is Michael. He's a friend. Is that a problem?"

"Frankly, with the election so close, it is. How do you think it would look if the man responsible for controlling crime in the city can't control his own woman?"

Emily stopped and pulled her hand from Phillip's. "I don't know what you think is going on here, but I am not *your woman*." She exhaled sharply. "And I don't need to be controlled."

Phillip wrinkled his brow as if this were a revelation. He cleared his throat. "What I meant was—"

"You were *informed*? Have you been spying on me?"

"Emily, dear, I didn't mean to upset you. The fact is, I'm a public figure, and I... we... must be sensitive to the image we project."

"It's obvious you know all about sensitivity."

"I think you're overreacting."

"I don't think *I'm* the one who's overreacting."

"All I ask is that, at least for the time being, you're not seen with this friend of yours in public."

"I'm not going to stop seeing Michael," she declared. "God, Phillip, you make it sound like I'm doing something wrong. I'm walking with him, not sleeping with him. And even if I were..."

They walked in silence.

"I'm tired," Emily said after a few moments. "I'd like to go home now."

Emily turned and started back toward the restaurant. For someone who was supposedly so intelligent, Phillip had found a way to ruin an otherwise perfect evening.

At eleven o'clock the next morning, Emily's doorbell rang. She laughed when she opened door. It appeared as if a huge bunch of flowers had walked up to her doorstep. The large arrangement concealed the delivery person from the waist up. She asked him to carry them inside and set them on the dining room table, hoping it would support the weight. She opened the card:

I noticed these in a shop window. They were stunning. They reminded me of you. Please forgive my insensitivity. Phillip.

She leaned over and inhaled slowly. *God, they smell beautiful.* She had to give Phillip kudos. If you're going to act like a jerk once in a while, knowing how to apologize is important.

CHAPTER **EIGHTEEN**

Three weeks passed and, other than his meetings with Emily in the park, Michael spent most of his time working on the new book. He found the writing process difficult. It dredged up painful memories of what he'd lost—what he'd let slip through his fingers. At the time, it seemed like too much work to maintain their relationship. Now, he spent considerably more time and energy trying to get it back.

Michael continued to see Emily. Occasionally, she brought Bogey and the three of them walked together like old times. Michael and Emily talked effortlessly about anything and everything. Before long, they finished each other's sentences like an old married couple. Michael impressed Emily with his perceptive insights.

"Good morning, Emily." Michael approached the Overlook railing with one hand behind his back.

Emily leaned on the railing and stared at the reflection of the low clouds in the gray water. She turned at the sound of his voice and smiled unconvincingly.

Michael approached and presented her with a single red rose.

"What's this for?"

"One month ago today, the most beautiful woman I've ever met walked into my book signing."

Emily looked from the rose to Michael, and cried.

"Not exactly the reaction I was going for."

"I'm sorry." She swiped at the tears that rolled down her cheeks.

"What's the matter, Em?" he asked in a soft voice. "Did something happen?"

"No." She took the rose, closed her eyes, and smelled it. Michael waited. "Richard gave me a single rose on our one-month anniversary, then added another every month for the first year."

"He doesn't sound like such a bad guy."

"He had his moments." She brushed away a tear. "Right now, I can't make up my mind whether I'm sad or angry—whether I miss him or wish I'd killed him myself."

Her words felt like a dagger in his heart.

Michael put his arms around her. Emily buried her face in his chest and sobbed. He said nothing, grateful to hold her for the first time in months. Tears welled in his own eyes. He didn't want to let go. Ever.

They stood for a few moments in silence. Emily raised her head to see the wet spot her tears had left on Michael's shirt. She pulled back just enough to wipe it with her free hand, as if that might remove it. "I'm sorry."

"Don't be." He gazed into her eyes, certain that something transpired between them at that moment. It happened in an instant—maybe only a fraction of an instant. He wondered if she'd felt it, too.

"Let's get some coffee," he suggested. "We could talk about it… or not. It's up to you."

"Okay. I don't want to stay here any longer."

"I'll buy you breakfast if you're feeling up to it."

Emily nodded.

"Come on." He slipped his arm around her, and they left the Overlook together.

Michael held the door open for Emily and followed her inside. Maggie's Diner resembled an old railroad car, long and narrow, with a counter along one side and retro-style booths along the other. The food was great and, in Michael's opinion, they made the best coffee in town.

A waitress behind the counter greeted them and told them to sit wherever they liked. Michael chose a booth at the end of the row. A handful of customers remained after the breakfast rush, and he nodded politely to a couple as he passed their booth. A folded newspaper sat on the table and he moved it out of the way before they both slid into their seats.

"Are you hungry?" he asked.

"I think I'll just have coffee."

A waitress came over and Michael ordered two coffees.

Emily touched the back of his hand. "Thank you for doing this."

"You looked like you could use a distraction."

"This is exactly what I needed," she said when their coffee arrived.

He added a splash of cream and stirred. He tapped the spoon on the edge of the cup when he finished. "Nothing like drowning your sorrow in a good cup of coffee."

"I'm sure there are those who say alcohol works better."

"Perhaps, but I think I'll just stick with coffee for now." He smiled.

Emily studied him. "You're a good man, Michael." Their eyes met. "For someone of such celebrity... you're really down-to-earth... more in touch with your feelings than most men I meet."

In touch with my feelings? I've never heard that one before. If you only knew who you were talking to. "My wife would have disagreed. She once told me she didn't think I had any."

"Perhaps she didn't know you as well as she thought."

"Perhaps," he said, taking another sip of coffee to hide a smile. He decided to stop before he said anything that might get him in trouble later.

Thanks to Rhonda falling on her sword—or more precisely, the DA's sword—Emily couldn't place Michael Riordan at the accident. She would see him as a handsome, successful, and perhaps charming author, rather than the drunk who killed her husband. His innocent charade suddenly sounded more sinister, and he shuddered involuntarily. Could he risk telling her the truth?

Michael sighed. "When I found you crying in the park, were you thinking about your husband?"

"Yes," she admitted. "We were married twenty-three years." The tears returned, and she looked away.

The bell above the door hijacked his attention. Two policemen entered. One he recognized as Tommy McKenna.

Tommy walked in like he owned the place and flirted with the waitress behind the counter. Michael watched him from the corner of his eye. His partner scanned the room. Neither of them sat down. Fortunately, Emily's back faced them.

Michael moved a little closer to the window, so Emily's body might block Tommy's view if he happened to look their way. He didn't want to take the chance that Tommy knew Michael Riordan.

Tommy said something to his partner, patted him on the shoulder, and walked toward their table. Emily brushed away tears, unaware that her brother was fifteen feet behind her and closing in fast. This wasn't going to go well.

CHAPTER **NINETEEN**

Michael panicked. He remembered the first time he met Emily's older brother.

Emily introduced her new boyfriend, Richard, to her parents while Tommy watched from the corner like a Pit Bull at the end of its chain. After the customary parental hugs and handshakes, Tommy pulled Richard aside.

"What makes you think you're good enough to date my baby sister?"

"You'll have to ask her."

Tommy leaned in and snarled. "If I ever see her cry because of something you said or did, I'm gonna rip your head off and stuff it down the hole in your neck." He paused for a second. "Comprende?"

Richard nodded. Tommy took a step back and pointed two fingers at his own eyes, then pointed them at Richard to say: I'm watching you.

"Hey, Sis," Tommy said when he reached their booth. He glanced at Michael then back to his sister. "What's wrong?"

At first, Emily didn't answer.

Michael stared at the black-and-white-checkered tile floor. Please say something, he thought.

"I'm okay," she finally replied, and wiped another tear before looking up.

"Is this guy bothering you?" Tommy looked sideways at Michael, and then back to Emily.

"No," she said. "He's a friend."

"You're sure you're okay?"

"Yes, Tommy. You can go now," she said calmly.

"I'll be right over there at the counter." He turned to Michael, and his eyes became little slits. "If you need anything, just holler." The words were meant for Emily, the message for Michael.

"I said I was okay."

Tommy turned and walked back to the counter, said something to his partner, and they sat.

"Richard and I used to go up to the Overlook."

Michael's eyes alternated between Emily and Tommy. "I know."

"What?"

He looked at Emily. "I mean... I know how difficult it must be."

Michael stretched out both arms and laid them across the table. Emily studied him for a moment and placed her hands in his.

"I'm sorry that you have to go through something like this. I know it's not easy," he said.

She stared at their hands. "I guess that's why I was there today." She hesitated for a moment before she looked up at him. "I'm glad you showed up when you did."

"Me, too," he said. "It must be a sad place for you now."

"I can handle the sadness." Her expression hardened. "I wish that's all it was."

"I don't understand."

She let go of his hands to wipe another tear. "I found out after he died that he'd been unfaithful. I had suspected it, but I didn't want to believe it unless I found proof."

He hated himself for what she was going through—what he had put her through. She deserved to know the truth. "What kind of proof?" he asked.

"What?"

"You said you had proof. What was it?"

"He lied to me." She twisted a few strands of hair around her finger. "I hate lies."

Michael avoided her stare. He'd lied to everyone, including Emily. He wondered how she would feel when she learned the truth. Perhaps he had waited too long. He stole a glance at the counter where Tommy sat.

"My sister saw them out to dinner one night."

"What?" Michael realized he hadn't been paying attention. "Did you say *your sister* saw them?"

Emily nodded. "He told me he had to work."

That must be what Samantha wanted me to tell her.

Emily continued. "Then after he died, I found a letter from the woman he was seen with. She claimed to be having an affair with Richard. She said he bought her expensive gifts with money from our savings. Apparently, she backed out when he surprised her with plane tickets for them to fly away together. She claimed she wasn't a home wrecker—even paid back all the money he'd spent."

She stopped to take a deep breath.

He read that letter at Carolyn's house when she threatened to blackmail him. He remembered shoving it in his pocket—no doubt where it had been found after the accident. Despite the tension, he laughed. "That's quite a story."

She glared at him like he'd just spit in her cup. "It's not funny, Michael."

"I'm sorry, but I think it is." He leaned back in his seat. "Well, maybe not funny, but it's pretty bizarre, wouldn't you say?"

She scrutinized him, her expression unreadable.

"C'mon, Emily. What kind of woman accepts expensive gifts and then when she starts to have second thoughts—if she has second thoughts—pays back the money? What did she do... mail you a check?"

"No." The muscles in her face tightened. "She gave it to Richard and he put it back in our account."

"How do you know that?"

"She said so in the letter."

The fry cook called out to the waitress and Michael turned his head. He took a long sip of coffee. A memory surfaced.

Richard stood facing Carolyn in her living room. A clock chimed on the mantle, and he glanced at it.

"You had no trouble accepting my offer in the first place," Carolyn said with an accusatory look.

"I wasn't thinking straight at the time. But I'm here to tell you I can't keep your money, and that this," he pointed at Carolyn and then to himself, "isn't going to happen."

"I'm sorry, lover boy, but I think it's a little late for that." Her eyes narrowed and her tone hardened.

"So, this is how you want to play it?"

"No, Richard. This is not how I want to play it, but you leave me no choice." She reeked of danger now. "You're not going to have much of a chance with her after she reads this." She pulled a folded piece of paper from her pocket.

"What's that?"

She held it in front of her. "Why don't you come see for yourself?"

Richard snatched it from her hand and took a few steps back before he unfolded it.

A smile crossed Carolyn's lips as she watched him read.

Michael's hand trembled. He set his cup down and turned his attention to Emily.

"Perhaps she offered him a way out and he took it." Michael took advantage of an opportunity to explain, even if disguised as a hypothetical story. "He put the money back in the account, but there were strings attached. What if he's the one who had second thoughts? Maybe he realized it would be better to tell you than to end up in Carolyn's debt and do something to hurt you. Maybe she shows him the letter—tries to blackmail him. What if he's on his way over to your place to come clean when he has the accident?"

Emily remained silent for a moment. Michael watched her wheels turn. For now, he just needed to open the door a crack.

"How did you know her name was Carolyn?"

"What?"

"I don't think I ever mentioned her name."

Michael squirmed. "I think you did." He wanted to tell her the truth, but with Tommy nearby, this wasn't the time or the place.

Emily frowned and waited for more. When it didn't come, "How do you explain what Samantha saw at the restaurant?"

"What did Richard have to say about it?"

She looked out the dirty window at the cars that passed by. She sighed. "I never got the chance to ask him."

"Tried and convicted without an opportunity to tell his side of the story?"

"I don't think I like what you're insinuating." She turned to face him again. "I'm not the bad guy here."

"All I'm saying is, if I had a wife as beautiful and charming as you, I'd want to hang on with both hands."

Emily twirled a few strands of her hair around her finger while she stared past him.

Michael noticed Tommy and his partner get up to leave. He made eye contact. Tommy pointed first with two fingers at his own eyes and then at Michael.

Message received. Michael looked back at Emily, hoping she hadn't noticed his distraction. *This is not good, he thought.* He tried to conceal his growing anxiety. Not good at all.

CHAPTER **TWENTY**

Michael returned home, unable to shake the image of Tommy's gesture before he left the diner. Just what I needed, he thought. As if the idea of Emily dating a political heavyweight and arguably the most eligible bachelor on the planet wasn't enough, now a Pit Bull stood in his path.

Angie, head in the refrigerator, looked up when Michael entered the room.

He dropped his keys on the counter. "What are you doing?"

"What does it look like I'm doing? I'm hungry."

Michael quickly closed the refrigerator door. He glanced at the sink for another broken wine bottle. "I thought you lived out back."

"I love you, too, Michael." She popped open a can of Dr. Pepper. "By the way, you need to do some shopping."

"I've been busy."

"It's not like you have to go to the store or anything. Just make a list and call Marion."

"Marion?"

"Yeah. She does all the shit you don't like to do, like shopping and cleaning. Her number's in your phone."

"And you're just telling me this now?"

A faint smile played on her lips. "Like you're the only one who's busy."

Angie thumbed through a stack of mail on the kitchen table.

"Anything for me?" Michael asked with a sardonic grin.

She held up what appeared to be an invitation. "You're going to Kevin's wedding, right?"

"Probably not." He shrugged. "Who's Kevin?"

"Only the coolest cousin ever." She paused, and her expression fell. "Seriously? You two were close. You really don't remember?"

Another shrug.

"You have to go." She looked him up and down. "But first, you need some new clothes."

"What's wrong with my clothes?"

She set the mail on the table. "You need to bring your A-game. There's bound to be some eligible bachelorettes at this wedding."

"I'm not looking for women."

"Okay. I'm sure there'll be some single dudes there, too."

"That's not what I meant." He paused while he considered how much to tell her. "I met someone at the book signing."

"Didn't I tell you those events were chick magnets?" Angie smiled with a triumphant nod. "Why don't you ask her?"

"I just met her. I can't ask her to a wedding."

"Fine. We're back to the bachelorettes."

"I'm more worried about the family. I don't remember anyone."

"No problem. You can wear a big bandage on your head." She stifled a laugh. "They'll forgive you."

He played along. "Won't that hurt my chances with the women?"

"It might actually help. Damaged men seem to get all the attention these days."

She had an answer for everything.

"We're going shopping," she said.

"Now?"

"I'll drive."

Michael threw his hands in the air.

"You can thank me later."

He shook his head in defeat. "I'll get my keys."

Angie picked up her purse and slung it over her shoulder. "Don't bother. I have a set."

Michael sighed. "Why am I not surprised?" he whispered as he followed her out the door.

Michael stood in front of a large mirror dressed in an expensive suit. Angie nodded her approval from a nearby chair while a tailor busied himself with a tape measure.

She held up two neckties. "Do you like the red or the blue?"

"You're the fashion expert."

She handed him the blue tie and he held it to his neck. He studied himself in the mirror and nodded. "Not bad."

Michael's smile turned to a frown when he caught a reflection in the mirror. The man from the park watched him through the store window. Michael turned around, but the man was gone.

"What's the matter?"

Michael held out his hand. "Uh... let me try the red one."

Angie helped him tie it while he stared, brow furrowed, at nothing in particular.

Emily and Samantha sat at a sidewalk table in front of their favorite cafe. A warm breeze swirled beneath the large striped awning. Emily pushed back the hair that had blown across her face and tucked it behind her ear.

"I still don't know why a man like Phillip Morgan would pick you over me," Sam said in playful protest. "We were both there. He must have had too much to drink."

"As I recall…" Emily flashed a smile. "He was stone sober."

Sam picked up her cup. "It must have been that sleazy push-up bra."

"Just a small part of my irresistible charm."

"So, what's this Mom tells me about some other guy you're seeing. A famous author?"

The breeze picked up the edge of Emily's napkin, and she tucked it under her empty plate. "Mom's got a big mouth."

"You could share the wealth with your favorite sister."

"You're my only sister."

"That's what I meant."

"Okay. I'll stop at two. The third one's yours."

Sam's expression turned serious. "Do you ever think about Richard?"

Of course she still thought about Richard. What kind of question was that? He'd been her first love. They'd been married for twenty-three years and had a beautiful daughter. But it ended in betrayal. That mark will never go away. How could anyone expect her to move on with people bringing it up all the time.

"If he were still alive, we'd probably be separated. I've moved on." Emily lifted her cup and stopped before taking a sip. "Isn't that what you've been telling me to do?"

"Well, yeah, but I hoped you'd take me with you."

Emily's raised eyebrow came with no comment.

A man walked by the table and Samantha paused. "What's the author like?" she asked after he passed.

"Michael? He's nothing like Phillip, but he's kind of… charming in his own way."

"You're literally dating Prince Charming. How can you even say that?"

Emily watched the traffic for a moment. "This will probably sound weird, but he reminds me of Richard."

"What happened to moving on?"

"Richard wasn't always that bad. Certainly not in the beginning."

Sam waited for her to add something more. When she didn't, she said, "So, what are you gonna do?"

"I don't know."

"Just pick one and send the other my way."

Emily dismissed her comment like she'd done a thousand times before. "I plan to ask Phillip to be my plus-one at a wedding in a couple of weeks."

"That should turn some heads." She moved to the edge of her chair and rested her elbows on the table. "Does that mean I get the author?"

CHAPTER **TWENTY-ONE**

Dreams haunted Michael throughout the night. Dreams or memories? He played back the pieces that he could remember.

Just when his relationship with Emily began to heat up, she cooled off without warning. It didn't make sense, like an ice storm on a hot July afternoon. And what's with the man in the Red Sox cap? Are the two things somehow connected? Clearly, he was being followed, but why? Did it have something to do with Tommy? Phillip? Perhaps a new obstacle had been put in his path by whomever conspired to keep him away from Emily.

The wedding he'd agreed to attend that afternoon seemed like nothing more than a waste of time, a distraction from his primary mission. He'd been spinning his wheels with Emily lately. They'd been together only once in the past two weeks. Their relationship needed to gain some traction before it spun out.

Michael sat at his desk and flipped through his notebook, a half-eaten ham sandwich on a plate next to him. B.B. King sang the blues from the stereo in the living room, the volume turned up to eleven. The morning had passed slowly, weighed down by thoughts of Tommy, the Red Sox fan, and his last conversation with Rhonda. In addition, he somehow had to break the news to Angie that he wouldn't be attending the wedding with her.

When B.B. stopped in the middle of a lyric, Michael stood and headed toward the living room.

"Jeezus, Michael," Angie said a little too loudly. "I thought you lost your memory, not your hearing."

When he reached the doorway, he stopped in his tracks. Somehow, his pain-in-the-ass little sister had turned into a beautiful woman. He'd never seen her in makeup before, let alone that little red dress and heels.

"You're…"

She struck a pose. "A woman?"

"Who are you, and what have you done with Angela?"

She hiked up her dress and yanked at the top of her pantyhose. "I'll be lucky if I make it through the first hour in this crotch basket."

"Aaaand… we're back."

"I need to borrow some toothpaste." She adjusted her dress.

"You've got your own toothbrush, right?"

Angie flashed a tight smile before a wary frown. "How come you're not dressed?"

"I've decided not to go."

"What? You *have* to go. It's the best place on earth to find a woman. Most of the single ones get trashed. It's easy pickins'."

"In case you hadn't noticed, I'm not that guy."

"That's right. You're the guy who writes about stuff instead of doing it."

"Don't you have a wedding to go to?"

"You're coming with me. Go put on that new suit. And don't forget your dancin' shoes."

"I don't want to go stag."

"Jeezus, Michael. Maybe you should have thought about that while you still had time to ask someone."

"Who would I have asked?"

"Seriously? What's the matter with you? You're handsome, successful, and borderline-charming when you want to be." She snorted. "There's plenty of women who'd cut off a toe to be on your arm."

He wasn't interested in plenty of women.

"What about that woman you met at the last book signing?"

Michael shrugged. "I've seen her a couple of times, but she's not returning my calls at the moment."

"So, you got dumped. Shit happens. There's plenty of other fish in the sea."

"I didn't get dumped."

"You say tomato…"

"For your information, I don't like fishing."

"What's not to like? You don't even have to throw out your line. You flash those baby blues, and they jump right into your boat. It happens all the time. Hell, if you weren't my brother—"

Michael held out his hands. "Stop right there."

Angie disappeared down the hall. She returned a few moments later holding a tube of toothpaste. "I'd love to stay and chat, but my date will be here soon."

"You have a date?" He feigned disappointment. "I thought you said we could…"

"You just stood me up. Good thing I had a backup plan, isn't it?" She exhaled. "Just because you want to waste your life, doesn't mean I shouldn't get a little—"

"Okay!" He held up his hands again. "I get it."

"I don't think you do." Her voice softened. "I'm trying to help you, Michael, but you have to work with me."

"Look, I appreciate your help, but there are a few things *you* don't understand."

"Jeezus, Michael. Just go get dressed." Her frustration boiled up and she tugged at her waist, apparently adjusting her under garments again.

"I thought you had a date."

"You're not going with me." She pointed at the staircase. "You're going to go upstairs, put on your big-boy pants, and drive yourself over to the church. Then you're going to suck it up and have a good time at the reception."

Michael studied her for a moment. He decided this was not a battle he wanted to fight. "You know what this means, don't you?" He didn't wait for an answer. "I'll have to sit at the losers' table."

A faint smile played on Angie's lips. She shrugged. "If the shoe fits…"

CHAPTER **TWENTY-TWO**

"Maybe you should wait someplace else," Angie said when she found Michael sitting on a stool at the reception hall bar.

"Maybe you should take your own advice."

She folded her arms and watched him order a club soda. "You look nice, Michael. Go mingle. Maybe you'll get lucky."

"I'm good."

"Are you sure you're going to be okay?"

"You better get back to your date before *he* gets lucky."

Angie hesitated, then pointed with two fingers at her own eyes and then at Michael. The gesture sent a chill down his spine. Angie turned and disappeared into the gathering crowd.

Michael looked past the rows of bottles arranged in front of a large mirror along the back of the bar and studied his reflection. He hoped someday to get used to the face that stared back. It didn't seem likely.

"Michael?" a familiar voice drifted in over his right shoulder.

He turned. Emily stood alone by his side. The scent of her perfume brought back memories from another life. It made him dizzy and, for a moment, unable to think straight. *Say something.*

"What are you doing here?" she asked with a confused expression.

"Of all the gin joints in all the towns in all the world, you walk into mine," he replied in his best Humphrey Bogart voice.

Emily laughed and set her purse on the bar. "I came to Casablanca for a wedding. I didn't expect to find you here."

She remembered. Okay, relax. He took a deep breath. *This is Emily, the woman you lived with for twenty-three years, not some blind date.* She appeared genuinely happy to see him. Perhaps, she hadn't been avoiding him, after all.

Michael signaled the bartender. "A glass of Pinot Noir for the lady, and I'll have another club soda."

"You're not drinking?"

"Trying to cut back."

The bartender set her glass on the bar. Emily eyed him curiously. "This is my favorite."

Michael watched her take a sip, and his mind went back to Richard's apartment some twenty-four years ago.

Emily sat next to him on the sofa with a glass of wine. They watched the end of Casablanca, an open bottle of Pinot on the coffee table.

Emily turned to Richard with a line from the movie. "Can I tell you a story, Rick?"

"Does it have a wow finish?" he said in his Humphrey Bogart voice.

"I don't know the finish yet."

"Go on. Tell it. Maybe one will come to you as you go along."

Richard seized the moment. He got down on one knee, pulled a small, velvet-covered box from his pocket, and flipped it open.

"Here's looking at you, kid... for the rest of my life." He paused to catch the breath that had escaped with the words. "Will you marry me?"

Emily didn't hesitate. "Yes!"

She wrapped her arms around Richard's neck and knocked him to the floor where they shared a long kiss.

Emily set her glass on the bar. "Bride or groom?"

Michael stared, lost in the memory.

"Earth to Michael..."

"What? Oh... uh, groom." He paused to regain his bearings. "Kevin is Michael's, uh, my cousin. You?"

"Sarah's a friend from work."

Michael downed the rest of his drink. "I'm glad you showed up. You're about the only person here I know."

Emily glanced around the room, then tilted her head. "You must have family here."

"Uh... yes. Of course." He raised his glass to his lips. He realized it was empty and set it down quickly. "It's just that I haven't seen most of them in... forever." He ordered another drink.

He spoke again after an awkward silence. "I haven't seen you in the park lately..."

"Michael." She looked down at her glass. "You know I—"

"Yeah, I know." He didn't try to hide his disappointment. "But, hey, we're just two friends who happened to meet at a wedding reception, right? Where's the harm in that?"

"There isn't any, I guess." She smiled and raised her glass. He brought his up to meet hers and they both took a drink.

He looked her up and down. "You clean up nice."

"Excuse me?"

"Uh… what I meant was... you know... I've only seen you in the park, and... it's just that you look… fantastic."

She smiled but said nothing.

Real smooth, he thought. "I'm sorry, I haven't done this in a while…"

"What... talk?" she asked with a grin.

"Talk to a beautiful woman." He held her gaze.

Emily blushed before looking away. "Thank you, Michael. You're sweet. I was going to say the same about you."

"That I'm a beautiful woman?" He looked down at his clothes and smoothed his tie with his hand. "That wasn't exactly the look I was going for."

Emily laughed. He remembered how he loved to make her laugh. He missed that.

They laughed together.

"You don't look so bad yourself," she said when their laughter subsided.

"This old thing?" He glanced at her sideways "I'm surprised the bride's people let you in here looking that good."

Emily's cheeks flashed a soft red. "Are you alone?"

"Just me. How about you?" He held his breath and waited for her answer. When she didn't reply, he said, "I'm waiting for Victor Lazlo to waltz in here and steal you away."

Emily smiled momentarily before her expression fell. She stared at the glass of wine in front of her. "That was Richard's favorite movie. I couldn't even tell you how many times we watched it together."

"I'm sorry. No more Casablanca talk."

She put her hand on his arm. "I'll be fine," she said, looking at him with those eyes.

Michael met her gaze, holding it as long as he could before he had to look away.

"He probably doesn't deserve it, but I still miss him from time to time." She took another drink. A silence descended upon them.

"So," he said. "You didn't answer my question."

"Which question was that?"

"You're obviously here alone. Where is Prince Phillip?"

"He had a previous engagement." She paused. "He's very important, you know."

Sarcasm, or perhaps even disdain, resonated in her voice. *What's this? A tiny crack in the Prince's armor?* "His loss."

A voice came over the PA system to inform them that the wedding party had arrived, and all guests should take their seats.

Michael glanced toward the reception hall door, then offered his hand to Emily. "Since you're without a proper escort, would you do me the honor?"

She accepted it with a cautious smile. "This doesn't mean anything."

CHAPTER **TWENTY-THREE**

They ate dinner and talked like old friends. Michael couldn't imagine how the day could get any better. In Michael's eyes, Emily was the only other person in the room. It seemed like a lifetime ago, and perhaps it was, but he was falling in love with her all over again.

He studied her and noticed that she hadn't changed much in twenty-five years. Tiny laugh lines had begun to appear at the corners of her eyes and strands of gray threaded her dark hair along her hairline, but it only made her more attractive— much like the taste of a fine wine that improves with age.

The band played an old tune that had been one of their favorites, and without thinking, he asked her to dance. Emily hesitated before she took Michael's hand. They were cautious at first, but soon he held her close. Neither one spoke. He held her in his arms while they swayed to the music. Halfway through the love song, he sensed the lyrics made her feel a bit uncomfortable.

"Did I mention that I'm glad you're here?" he said.

Emily smiled without words.

"I'd look pretty stupid dancing alone to *this* song."

Emily flashed an almost flirtatious smile. He considered her mixed signals, and his eyes narrowed.

Whenever they'd danced to this song in the past, he'd always stolen a kiss at the end. The thought crossed his mind. Perhaps the only thing that held him back was the image of her running for the parking lot if he did. He had to remind himself that, while he held the woman with whom he'd spent most of his life, Emily was in the arms of a virtual stranger. Nothing could have prepared him for this.

Their movement slowed as the music faded, and they looked into each other's eyes. Time stood still. This is where he belonged. Many of the other guests moved toward their seats, but Michael and Emily held each other's gaze. Their heads moved a little closer, eyes still locked.

The music resumed with an upbeat tempo and their moment vanished. They silently agreed to return to their seats as other couples approached the dance floor.

Michael sat down while Emily excused herself and picked up her purse. He watched her disappear into the crowd. After a couple of deep breaths to restore his normal heart rate, he walked to the bar.

Emily returned shortly after he did. She thanked him for the glass of wine and continued on like nothing had happened. Soon Michael found himself relaxed and having the best time he'd had since... well, he couldn't remember. The band had taken a break and Emily laughed at one of Michael's jokes while a man in an expensive suit walked toward them. The man stopped behind Emily and put his hands on her shoulders.

Emily looked up at him. "Phillip," she said, an element of surprise in her voice. "I thought you weren't able to make it." She shot a nervous glance at Michael, then back at Phillip.

"Hello, darling," he said and leaned over to kiss her on the cheek.

Michael looked away. When he turned back, Emily wore a guilty expression, like she'd been caught doing something wrong. We were just sitting here, he thought. Does Phil have her on that short a leash?

Phillip straightened up. "I ducked out early. I knew you would be the most beautiful woman here." He glanced at

Michael. "I couldn't risk one of the other guests stealing you away."

Michael forced a smile. *Great! Rich AND charming.* I think I'm going to be sick.

"This is my friend Michael," Emily offered.

Phillip looked sideways at Emily. She glared back. He extended a hand to Michael with a counterfeit smile. "Phillip Morgan, Assistant District Attorney."

Assistant Jackass is more like it, he thought. He stood and reluctantly shook the man's hand. "Michael Riordan."

The color drained from Phillip's face. "Michael Riordan..." Phillip glanced at Emily and repeated the name. He turned to Michael. "What do you do?"

"I'm a writer."

"I mean for a living."

"So do I," Michael said as calmly as he could.

"Anything I might have read?"

"I don't know. Can you read?"

Phillip's arrogant eyes narrowed.

"I've only written one book. It's called *Chance of a Lifetime*, and it's about this writer who meets a pretty girl at a wedding while her boyfriend is out playing golf."

Emily stifled a laugh.

Phillip's back stiffened. "I read that one. It doesn't end well for the writer."

The two locked eyes for a moment. "Well, I should probably get going," Michael said, then turned to Emily with a slight bow. "Thank you for the dance."

Emily's eyes widened, and she flashed a quick smile. Phillip frowned. He opened his mouth to speak, but before he could say anything, Michael turned and headed for the bar.

The first glass of Scotch went down too easily, and he sat with his back against the bar and ordered another. Emily and

Prince Phillip talked at their table, and he would have given anything to listen in on their conversation. He wondered how many times she'd seen him and how serious they'd become. He watched Emily steal a glance in his direction every now and then.

Michael knew who Phillip Morgan was. Anyone in Springfield who owned a television or read a newspaper knew him—Springfield's golden boy on a fast track to the DA's office. He took advantage of every opportunity to get his face in front of potential voters. Now, it appeared he was on a fast track to get into Emily's pants. That is, if he hadn't been there already. The thought made Michael's blood boil. He turned around and ordered another drink, unable to watch any longer.

After a few minutes, he set his empty glass on the bar and stood, planning to go to their table and give that pompous ass a piece of his mind. He'd only taken a couple of steps when they stood and walked toward the dance floor. He turned and headed for the men's room.

When he returned, he ordered another drink and searched for the couple on the dance floor. They weren't hard to find. Phil must have noticed all the video cameras because he hammed it up. Emily floated around the dance floor with Fred Astaire in an Armani suit. She appeared to enjoy herself.

Michael took another drink, disappointed in his behavior. *Way to go, Michael. That was charming. Don't let him get to you.* He finished his drink, pulled out his wallet, and dropped a couple bills on the bar.

CHAPTER **TWENTY-FOUR**

Michael, who was in no condition to drive, made it home safely in spite of himself. The evening had gone well until that jackass Morgan showed up. He kicked off his shoes and fell onto the sofa. Five minutes later, the doorbell rang.

"Nobody's home," he called.

The bell rang again.

He rubbed his eyes with his fists and rolled off the sofa. "I'm coming."

When he reached the door, the bell rang again. When he reached the door, the bell rang again. He fumbled with the lock before pulling the door open.

Tommy's eyes widened. "You?"

"What do you want?" Michael asked abruptly.

"I was told to deliver a message." Tommy folded his beefy arms across his chest. "A good friend of mine did not... appreciate... your wise-ass remarks in front of his girl this evening."

HIS girl? "So, he sent one of his goons over here to scare me off?"

Tommy jabbed an index finger hard into Michael's chest. It pushed him backward into the room. Tommy followed him in. "That's right, tough guy."

Michael, still a little shaky from the alcohol, struggled to regain his balance.

"I had a feeling you were trouble when I saw you at the diner," Tommy growled. "Consider this your second warning."

Tommy was a couple of inches taller than Michael and outweighed him by thirty pounds, most of which appeared to be muscle.

"Emily is a friend of mine." Michael straightened up and stood his ground.

Tommy leaned in to create an uncomfortable space between them. "Not anymore." The words hissed through his teeth like Clint Eastwood in Dirty Harry.

Both men glared at each other.

"Comprende?"

Michael pointed toward the door. "Get the hell out of my house."

"Or what... you'll call the police?" Tommy snickered.

"Get out."

Slowly, Tommy turned to leave. He stopped when he reached the front porch. "You don't want me to have to come back here," he said and disappeared into the night.

Big, bad Tommy McKenna. A hired gun for a corrupt politician. A setback perhaps, but not enough to keep him away from Emily.

Something shattered outside. Tommy called from somewhere in the darkness. "You'd better get that tail light fixed. I'd hate to see you get pulled over."

Michael turned the deadbolt and exhaled sharply. He leaned back against the locked door. I never did like you very much, he thought, but I always gave you the benefit of the doubt—one of Springfield's finest, my ass. Turns out you're nothing but a two-bit thug. He watched through the peephole as Tommy drove away.

Michael walked into the study, stopped at his desk and placed one hand on the edge for support. He noticed the two-year coin on the desk where Angie had left it. He picked it up, glared at it briefly, and threw it across the room.

Note to self: Buy a bottle of Scotch.

Michael dragged himself out of bed the next morning, reminded of what can happen when one consumes too much alcohol. The few times Richard had overdone it in his lifetime didn't prepare him for what he felt at the moment. His brain seemed to have expanded overnight and pushed mercilessly against the inside of his skull. He debated whether to crawl back to bed or to split open his head and relieve the pressure. However, even with his diminished powers of reasoning, he decided on a third option, which was both quicker than the first and less lethal than the second.

Michael rummaged through the bathroom medicine cabinet and found a single ibuprofen tablet. This, of course, was unacceptable. Despite having slept in his clothes, he headed to the drug store to restock his medicine cabinet.

Michael, in dark sunglasses, set several bottles of pills and a bottle of water down on the drug store counter and rubbed his temples. He searched his pockets for cash while a line formed behind him. He pulled out a credit card and dropped it on the counter. On his way out of the store, he felt the stare of someone in line. He turned around. One man wore a blue baseball cap that reminded him of the man in the park. Michael hesitated, but decided he needed some pills and a mega-dose of caffeine before he could trust anything his brain might tell him.

He returned to his car, reached into the plastic sack, and pulled out the first two bottles he touched. He swallowed a couple of pills from each and washed them down with the water before he drove to Maggie's for a large coffee. He scanned the parking lot for Tommy's cruiser. The coast was clear. He settled into the back booth for a caffeine therapy session.

Michael walked a little lighter by the time he parked his car in his driveway. He slipped his key into the deadbolt and found it unlocked. He didn't recall leaving it unlocked, however, given the way he'd left the house, he couldn't be sure. He did a quick scan up and down the street and, when he found nothing out of the ordinary, pushed the door open a few inches. He paused to listen. Nothing.

Tommy McKenna had him on edge, and he hoped the thug hadn't paid him another visit. The thought sobered him. He slowly opened the door, and silently berated himself for not moving one of the baseball bats he'd found in the basement up to the hall closet.

He left the door ajar and crept silently into the living room, his senses on full alert. In the middle of the room, he stopped and looked around. Nothing seemed out of place. The clock ticked on the mantle. He realized he'd been holding his breath, and exhaled slowly.

A rustle in the kitchen sent a chill through his veins. He reached for the fireplace poker from the brass stand on the hearth. With shaking hand, he raised the makeshift weapon and wondered if he could really hit someone. He hoped he wouldn't have to find out.

Michael stood next to the kitchen door with his back against the dining room wall and listened again. Nothing. He rested his head against the wall and tried to slow his runaway heart. It hammered so loudly, he feared it might give away his position.

Tommy had threatened him less than twelve hours ago, and he'd been asleep for most of it. He hadn't had a chance to do anything that would warrant another visit.

CHAPTER **TWENTY-FIVE**

With weapon in hand, Michael thrust his head around the corner. He pulled it back quickly like he'd seen the detectives do on television. Before his brain could fully process what he'd seen, Angie, who sat at the kitchen table with a cup of coffee and a magazine, jumped up from her chair.

"Michael?" she called. "Is that you?"

Michael exhaled before he stepped into the kitchen. Angie held a rolled-up magazine in front of her like a sword.

"You scared the shit out of me." She lowered her paper weapon and focused her eyes on the fireplace tool in his hand. "What the hell are you doing?"

Michael's heart still hammered his chest. "I scared *you*?"

He set his weapon on the edge of the table and dropped his bag on the counter.

"You look like hell," she said.

"I didn't sleep well, but thanks for noticing." He pulled a glass from the cupboard and filled it with water.

"So, what's with the Rambo act?"

"I don't know." Michael swallowed a couple more pills and stared out the window above the sink. "I guess I thought you were someone else."

Angie pointed at the poker. "Really? What did you plan to do with that thing?"

He set the empty glass down in the sink and turned to face her. "I'm not sure, but I think I was going to crack your skull."

"You're doing it again, Michael, and I won't stand by and watch you—"

"Why are you here?"

"Come to a meeting with me."

Michael said nothing.

Disappointment washed over Angie's face.

"I'll think about it," he said to shut her up. "Now, what are you doing in my kitchen?"

"Mostly stealing your coffee." She sat and opened her magazine. "So, why didn't you introduce me to your friend at the wedding?"

She waited for a response. When none came, she added, "What I don't understand, is why she was dancing with Phillip Morgan."

"I don't want to talk about it."

"That's the first time I've seen him up close. Fancy suit, perfect hair… he's even hotter in person."

Michael glared. "You're not helping, Ang."

Angie picked up her coffee cup, grinning. "Did I mention his eyes?" She took a sip. "I'd do him in a heartbeat."

"Still not helping."

"I'm sorry." She attempted unsuccessfully to conceal her amusement. "So, are you going to tell me her name or not?"

"Her name's Emily."

"How did you two meet?"

We met at the campus pub twenty-five years ago.

"Michael?"

He realized he'd been staring at his ring finger. He looked up. "We met at a book signing."

Angie set her cup down, eyes wide. "She's the one? I can see why you…" She paused, brow furrowed. "I thought you said you didn't have a date."

"I met her there."

She pushed her glasses down and stared at him over the rims. "The woman you hit on at the book signing, the same one who dumped you a few weeks later, just happened to be at Kevin's wedding?"

"She's a friend of the bride."

"I think it's kismet."

"Tell that to Mr. Fancy Pants."

"I don't get it."

"Apparently, they're dating."

"Yikes! That could be a problem."

Michael's back stiffened.

"He's a catch, Michael. Even if she was crazy enough to let him go, that's gotta be a hard act to follow."

"I'm not going to let that blow-hard get in my way."

Angie walked to where Michael stood. She set her cup in the sink, then playfully elbowed Michael in his side. "Good luck with that, Rambo."

Tommy McKenna sat in his police cruiser outside Maggie's Diner while his partner Jason went inside to order a couple of breakfast sandwiches and coffee to go. Tommy did all the driving—and all the thinking, as far as he was concerned. Jason, who had been on the force only two years, made most of the food runs. Occasionally, Tommy offered to order the food if a pretty young waitress was inside. He favored three local eateries and tried to keep track of who worked each shift. He'd never been considered the sharpest knife in the drawer, but he paid attention to details when it came to women.

Tommy took care of some unofficial business at the onboard computer installed on the cruiser's console while

Jason flirted with a waitress at the counter. Tommy tapped R-i-o-r-d-a-n on the keyboard and pressed the Enter key.

He'd visited Riordan a few nights ago at Phillip's request. The fact that he'd been ordered off the property did not sit well, but he had to be careful when he was in uniform on unofficial business. He'd heard the name Michael Riordan before, but he couldn't quite put his finger on where or when. The name was familiar, but not in a good way.

Tommy was no stranger to background checks or off-the-books surveillance. He'd been doing as much with Emily's boyfriends since high school, but now he had the resources of the Springfield Police Department at his disposal.

Phillip had seemed nervous when he'd asked Tommy to pay Michael a visit. Whenever Phillip's considerable powers of persuasion weren't sufficient, the next step frequently involved Officer Thomas McKenna. The two had been good friends since they met when Tommy was in the Academy and Phillip was in Law School. Their friendship spawned a mutually beneficial relationship.

No records found appeared on the screen, and Tommy scratched his chin. Phillip never gets nervous. Something was up.

Jason set the cardboard tray with two cups of coffee on the roof and opened the passenger door. Tommy tapped a key to clear the screen. Jason tossed a bag in and handed him one of the cups before he sat down and closed the door.

The two officers ate in relative silence inside the idling car. Jason made several attempts to start up a conversation with an otherwise preoccupied Tommy.

"C'mon, man, something's eatin' you. What is it?" Jason asked.

"Nothing I can't handle." He shoved the last piece of breakfast sandwich in his mouth and washed it down with the rest of his coffee. "Let's get outta here."

CHAPTER **TWENTY-SIX**

Coiffed hair and sun-tanned faces floated on a sea of tuxedos and designer evening wear. Pretty little waitresses weaved their way through the crowd with trays of elegant hors d'oeuvres and sparkling champagne flutes. It appeared as if Emily had walked onto a movie set.

The fundraiser for Phillip's campaign looked like a who's-who of Springfield's elite. Emily had arrived on Phillip's arm to a round of applause and raised glasses. She'd been given specific instructions in the limo on how to act and what to say. They settled in, and he shook hands and smiled his winning smile. He didn't necessarily like these people or agree with their political views. He needed their money, so he worked the room like a pro.

In Emily's eyes, Phillip could be as two-faced as the rest of them. Maybe more. She hadn't yet seen this side of him and tried to dismiss the unsettling thought that it extended beyond the political theater.

An hour into the affair, Emily decided she'd had enough. She excused herself, grabbed another glass of champagne, and stepped out onto one of the balconies. The city lights, while picturesque, were no match for the billion stars that twinkled above on a purple canvas. She felt more than a little out of place. This was Phillip's world, and not one she would have chosen. Yet here she was. Ultimately, people make their own choices, so she had no one to blame but herself.

Her thoughts turned to Michael. She focused her gaze on the brightest star in the sky and wondered if he might be gazing at the same light. She admitted to herself that she'd been disappointed when Phillip showed up at the wedding. She'd felt comfortable in Michael's company, and a bit surprised with the ease of their conversation. He, too, was something of a celebrity, but what she knew of his world was nothing like what she'd seen tonight.

She recalled the awkward circumstances surrounding their first meeting, and she smiled. Michael didn't try to hide behind a cleaned and polished facade. His authenticity was refreshing, particularly after she'd had a taste of life in the political world.

"What are you doing out here?"

Phillip stood a few feet behind her on the balcony. Emily turned. She'd been gone for nearly a half-hour. Did he have difficulty finding her, or had he been unaware that she'd left his side? She turned back toward the city lights. "If you knew me, you wouldn't have to ask."

"Come back inside. I need you."

"For what? Arm candy?" Emily returned her gaze to the stars. "I thought I could do this, but… I don't like these people."

"Truth be told, I don't like most of them either." He tugged at his shirt sleeve and adjusted his cuff link. "But this is politics."

"Don't you ever get tired of it?"

"The sound of their money keeps me awake."

He stood by her side. She hung her head, and he placed a finger under her chin to lift it. He flashed his winning smile, and the edges of her frustration melted away, even as red flags went up in the back of her mind.

"Let's leave," she pleaded. "We'll go someplace quiet, away from all of… this."

"Emily, my dear, don't be naive. That's not an option."

She bristled at the word. The condescension in his voice intensified the sting.

"We need to get back inside," he said as if speaking to a child.

"I'll be right in." She raised her glass to her lips. Her arms labored under the weight of the jewelry Phillip had insisted she wear. "I just need a couple more minutes."

Phillip's glare scorched her skin. After a few awkward moments, he turned and walked inside. Emily pulled her phone from her purse and dialed.

Ice melted in two fingers of Scotch while Michael reclined in one of the poolside lounge chairs. He stared into the night sky, considering his next move. He couldn't shake the guilt that gnawed at the back of his mind. He hadn't been unfaithful as Emily believed, but in the human mind, perception is reality. He'd given her enough circumstantial evidence to support her conclusion, and Richard was no longer around to vindicate himself. Michael needed to find a way to convince her otherwise.

He took a drink and stared at Polaris, the North Star. Arguably the brightest star in the sky, ancient mariners used its light to guide them in their travels. He could use such a guide on his journey. Arthur had helped him take his first few steps, but the strange little man hadn't been around much lately.

Michael's phone vibrated against the glass under the umbrella of a large table ten feet away. The phone had become a source of annoyance lately. It rang day and night, calls from a long list of contacts whose names meant nothing. He thought he'd left the damn thing inside. The call went to voicemail.

CHAPTER **TWENTY-SEVEN**

Michael moved around the kitchen like a pro. Emily's voicemail message the previous night prompted a dinner invitation which she graciously accepted. Steak, twice-baked potatoes, and fresh asparagus were on the menu. Emily sipped a glass of Pinot while she watched Michael slice mushrooms at the island counter.

"I'm sorry about the wedding." She turned her glass in her hand. "That must have been awkward for you."

"He's a real charmer," Michael replied without looking up.

"Can we pretend it never happened?"

"Pretend what never happened?"

Emily smiled, then changed the subject. "I admire a man who knows his way around the kitchen. Richard could grill a steak with the best of them, but that was pretty much the extent of his culinary skills."

Michael pushed the mushrooms from the cutting board into the pan with the back of his knife. "That was me once, but I'm learning to expand my horizons." He dropped two thick steaks on the Jenn-Air.

"It smells great."

He'd been given a second chance, and he wasn't about to blow it. He'd done the shopping himself, then summoned Marion to clean the house and set a table worthy of the finest restaurant. He stopped just short of hiring a waiter to serve the meal and a violinist to serenade them while they ate.

Michael pushed his empty plate away, pleased with the result of his efforts. Emily appeared to have enjoyed the meal and the conversation.

He set his empty wine glass on the table. "Well? How did I do?"

Emily smiled and offered a nod of approval. "Everything was fabulous."

"Are you ready for dessert?"

"There's more?" She leaned back in her chair. "Can we wait a bit?"

"Absolutely. I'll clear the table." He stood and gestured toward the living room. "You're welcome to wander. There's a great CD collection. Why don't you pick something out?"

Michael walked their plates into the kitchen while Emily perused the rack of disks in the living room. Music played a few minutes later while he stood in front of the open refrigerator. He stopped to listen and nodded his approval.

Bruce Springsteen sang *Dancing in the Dark* while Emily strolled around the room, admiring the artwork on the walls. She leaned her head inside an open door to an adjoining room. After a quick glance toward the kitchen, she stepped inside.

Michael's study provided an elegant space from which to practice his craft. Wood, stone, and plenty of glass surrounded her. She walked past a large antique desk to admire the back yard through a set of oversized French doors. The pool and the landscaping were beautiful, but the basketball court seemed a little out of place.

Two large bookcases flanked the stone fireplace that anchored the wall opposite the desk. Emily scanned some of the titles—classics, reference, and some newer fiction. A few old family photos shared the space. Apparently, Michael had a younger sister. Emily smiled at a faded photo from a Christmas morning long ago.

A little farther down, her eye caught a glimpse of a newer photo, and she froze. She picked it up and stared. *The little black dress.* Michael and the woman from the funeral stood side by side, all hugs and smiles. Emily didn't know what to think, but she had to admit it was a huge coincidence. She set the photo down slowly.

On her way back to the door, she stopped at Michael's desk. She picked up the notebook that sat on his closed laptop. Perhaps it contained information about his book. She glanced back at the bookshelves. The woman in the photo continued to watch her. She felt like an intruder poking around someplace where she didn't belong. Her eyes grew wider as she flipped through the pages.

"Dessert's ready," Michael called from the kitchen.

Emily returned the notebook to Michael's desk and joined him in the dining room.

Michael set two plates and a carafe on the table. His expression fell. "What's the matter, Em? You look like you just saw a ghost."

"I'm going to have to skip dessert."

"We can wait a little longer."

"I think I'd better just go home."

Michael frowned. "Is everything okay?"

She looked at him like she was about to say something, then turned away.

Everything was going so well, he thought while he stood on his front steps and watched her tail lights disappear into the night.

Michael sat in the dark beside the pool, phone to his ear. "It's Michael again. Please call me."

Michael watched the activity from a bench in Franklin Park. Emily had always been a creature of habit, and he didn't expect her to change just because Richard was gone. After the kids had moved out, Saturday mornings consisted of coffee and a light breakfast at Maggie's Diner followed by a walk in the park. The bench he sat on was on their normal route, and sometimes they'd stop there to rest if their light breakfast hadn't been so light.

After nearly an hour he stood and paced. Every time he made some real progress, something would spook her and she'd run. He had to figure out how to make her stay. He checked the time on his phone, shook his head, and left the park.

Michael sat in his car in the parking lot and watched people come and go. He pounded the steering wheel with both fists. He took a deep breath, started the car, and looked over his shoulder before backing out. A car pulled up behind him and blocked his path.

Tommy wore plain clothes and presumably drove his own car—like he had nothing better to do on his day off. He stared silently at Michael, whose heart nearly jumped out of his chest onto the seat next to him. Nevertheless, Michael refused to look away. He would not be intimidated. Finally, Tommy made his *I'm watching you* gesture and drove off.

Michael breathed again.

CHAPTER **TWENTY-EIGHT**

The Riverside Grill, situated along the scenic Algonquin River, had an outdoor dining area that overlooked the valley. Leaves had begun to change color, adding splashes of orange and gold to the panorama. Michael took a seat at one of the tables and waited. He needed a plan, something to turn things around, to keep her from slipping away.

Emily had reluctantly agreed to meet him for lunch. Phillip had a virtual restraining order against him with Tommy acting as his enforcer, so Michael decided that a trip out of town was a wise choice. The twenty-minute drive up Route 7 to Riverside offered just the right amount of buffer.

Emily arrived while he considered his next steps. He stood and welcomed her. She offered a nod and a quick smile before turning to take in the view.

"It's beautiful here," was all she said.

A waitress took their order, and they talked while they waited for the food to arrive. Their conversation lacked the same easy give-and-take to which he'd become accustomed. Emily remained guarded, hesitant to stray from simple, benign small talk. While the specter of Phillip Morgan loomed large, Michael sensed there was more to her withdrawal.

Emily gazed out over the river valley while the waitress set their plates on the table. "Richard talked about coming up here," Emily said after she left. "He had an old, I guess you'd call it classic, car he used to love to drive up this way. He'd stop somewhere for breakfast. It might have been this place." She sighed. "He never took me."

"I'm sure he regrets that." He took a bite of his sandwich. "What kind of car was it?"

"Mustang. Not sure of the year. Late sixties, I think. It needed a lot of work when he bought it, but he was pretty good with cars. He did most of the work himself." Disappointment washed over her face.

"You didn't like the car?"

"Oh, I liked it, it's just that..." Her voice trailed off.

"It's just that, what?"

She stopped eating. "Sometimes, I think he loved that car more than he loved me." Emily paused and held his gaze. "He even had a name for it. The Blue Knight. How stupid is that?"

Michael swallowed hard. "If the car was blue, it's not THAT stupid."

"Really? You're going to take his side?"

Michael looked away.

"There were nights when he'd be out in the garage making love to that damn car while I lie in bed alone," she said, her eyes fixed on the horizon once again.

Michael pictured her alone in their bed waiting for him, and his chest tightened. At the same time, the fact that she confided in him again gave him hope.

"And my brother, Frank... he didn't help. He's a pilot and flew them to car auctions all the time. Last year Richard spent my birthday at an auction in Jersey."

"I'm sorry."

"It's not your fault."

Michael set his sandwich down and swallowed hard. "I didn't know you felt like that."

She frowned. "What?"

"I mean... I... I just meant women in general."

A man walked by the table. "So, why are men so insensitive to such things?" she said after he passed.

"Hmmm. Loaded question." He took a deep breath. "I think men and women are just wired differently."

"That sounds like a cop-out."

"Perhaps it is. Perhaps we aren't willing to admit that we often let insignificant, material things get in the way of the more important things in life. In my experience, women are more likely to value the things you can't put a price on, such as love and family."

Emily studied him for a moment. "Good answer."

"Unfortunately, it appears I learned that lesson too late."

"Too late for what?" she asked.

"Too late to make a difference, I guess."

He watched her eat the last French fry, her gaze once again off in the distance.

She turned to him when she finished. "Weren't you the one who told me that it's never too late?" Their eyes locked, and he couldn't look away. Emily picked up her napkin and wiped the corner of her mouth. She raised her eyebrows impatiently.

"Yeah, I guess I was," he finally admitted. "So, let me ask you something..."

Emily shifted uncomfortably as if she regretted not ending the conversation when she had the chance.

"Why is it suddenly too late for us?"

She twirled a few strands of hair around her index finger and avoided his stare. "Michael, I ... I told you ... I like you, but you know I'm with Phillip," she said without looking up.

"How's that working out for you?"

He waited for a response which didn't come. She stood, picked up her empty plate, and walked away.

"Emily." He followed her.

She deposited everything in the trash barrel, then turned to face him.

"You and I have a connection," he continued. "I think you feel it, too. Otherwise, you wouldn't be here."

She stood motionless in front of him and held his gaze.

"I want to see more of you, not less," he moved a little closer. "I think you know that, but you choose to push me away."

Emily lowered her head. "Michael, don't."

Michael brought his hand up under her chin and gently lifted her head. She didn't resist. A few strands of hair blew across her face, and he brushed them back. Warmth surged in his chest as he leaned in, hoping she'd reciprocate.

At the last second, Emily turned her head. She hesitated for an instant then turned back to meet his lips. His mind let go of everything else. He wanted to stay in that moment forever.

She pulled back and studied him, searching for something.

"Emily?" he whispered.

She didn't respond and appeared to struggle with her thoughts for a moment before lowering her head. She stared at the ground. "I can't."

"What?"

She raised her head, but her eyes darted back and forth, avoiding his. "I have to go." She turned and walked toward the parking lot.

Michael watched her for a moment before following. "You need to be honest with yourself, Em. I know you felt it."

"Please don't call me anymore." She quickened her pace.

Michael caught up with her and blocked her path. "Tell me you didn't feel something powerful—something you can't explain. Make me believe that, and I'll disappear. I won't bother you again."

Emily covered her mouth with her hand. She pushed past him and walked briskly to her car.

Michael watched her drive off. He returned to his table. Other couples talked and laughed while they ate, and he had to look away.

As he stood to leave, he noticed a man watching him from one of the corner tables. Michael marched over to his table. The man with the Red Sox cap stared at him through dark sunglasses.

"Who the hell are you?" Michael demanded. "And why are you following me?"

The man smiled. "Sit down, Richard."

CHAPTER **TWENTY-NINE**

Michael stared at the stranger, his mouth agape.

The man leaned back and pointed to an empty chair. "Please… have a seat."

Michael sat slowly as he studied the man. He swallowed hard when the stranger removed his sunglasses.

"You're supposed to be..."

"Dead?"

"Where the hell are we?" Michael's eyes darted back and forth.

"We're not in Kansas anymore."

"I read that Carl Dunham died six years ago. It wasn't as sad a day as you might expect."

"Ouch."

"Let me guess. You met someone, got tired of her, and faked your death to get away."

"I didn't fake anything."

"If you're dead, does that mean that I'm…"

"That depends." He wrinkled his brow. "Is that what you want?"

"I didn't think I had a choice."

Carl folded his hands on the table and leaned in. "People near death often have an out-of-body experience. Some go back, others move on."

"If that's what this is, I need to go back."

"You can't just click your heels, Dorothy."

Michael frowned, but said nothing.

"You need a reason to live," he continued. "A singular, compelling reason."

"I have a reason."

"Look at you." He waved a hand in Michael's direction. "You're a wealthy man. Isn't that what Richard wanted?"

"Yeah, but..."

"That's not enough, is it? You want something else now. The very thing you were once willing to sacrifice."

"You're in no position to judge."

He ignored Michael's accusation. "So, what are you going to do about it?"

"When did you start to care about what I do?"

"Believe it or not, Son, I've always cared."

Michael closed his eyes. If that was true, he hadn't felt it. His father disappeared when he was twelve. Rumors surfaced about another woman.

"Well?"

Michael's pulse quickened and pounded in his neck. "I'm working on it."

"There's only a small window of opportunity."

"For what?"

"To show Emily who you really are and change her feelings toward you. Otherwise, I'm afraid there's no going back."

Michael chewed his bottom lip as he studied the man.

"You need to make some changes." Carl leaned back and folded his arms across his chest. "You can start by looking in the mirror."

"In case you hadn't noticed, there's someone else in the mirror now."

He looked at Michael for a moment, then sighed like he'd been trying to explain the theory of relativity to a child. "I'm not talking about what's on the outside."

Carl stood.

"Wait."

He paused, then put his hand on Michael's shoulder. "It's pretty arrogant to believe we always have tomorrow."

Arthur's warning echoed in his ears, and Michael hung his head. When he looked up again, his father was gone. An all-too-familiar feeling of panic grabbed hold of his chest. "That's right, just disappear again." he said to an empty chair. "Maybe you're the one who should look in the mirror."

People stopped eating and stared.

Michael took the long way home. He traveled down lonesome, two-lane country roads, his thoughts spinning faster than his wheels. He pushed it into fourth gear and pressed the pedal toward the floor. Houses and small farms bled into one another as they rushed past his window. The speedometer passed eighty and he squeezed the steering wheel.

"You need to make some changes," he mocked his father's words. "Don't you think I know that?"

Eighty-five.

He's full of advice now, he thought. Too little, too late. Where the hell was Carl Dunham when I needed him?

Ninety.

Richard frowned and tightened his grip. Only thinking about himself, that's where.

Ninety-five.

"What about me?" he yelled. A tear slid down his cheek.

One hundred.

He took his hand off the wheel for a second, and the car veered a little to the right. Speed amplified every movement. His tires bit into the gravel on the shoulder and he pumped the brakes. The speedometer needle fell, but the back end of the car fishtailed. Gravel flew. He wrenched the wheel and pumped the brakes again, struggling to regain control.

The needle passed fifty on its way down, and he jumped on the brake pedal. The car skidded to a stop sideways across the northbound lane. His heart beat in his throat as he backed the car onto the shoulder.

Richard climbed out of his car, walked around to the passenger side, and leaned back against the fender. He listened to the leaves rustle in the breeze. A crow's throaty call admonished him from a nearby tree.

Gravel crunched under the tires of a police cruiser that rolled up behind him. The officer jumped out like he'd just cornered a fugitive and ordered Michael to return to his vehicle. Michael hesitated, about to ask what he'd done, when the officer placed his hand on his gun and repeated the order. Michael complied. The officer approached after Michael slid into the driver's seat.

"I saw your little stunt," he said, and took Michael's license and registration back to his car.

A second cruiser with lights flashing approached from the opposite direction and executed a sharp U-turn, skidding onto the shoulder in front of Michael's car. The door swung open, and Tommy jumped out.

CHAPTER THIRTY

Tommy flashed a shit-eating grin when he walked past Michael's window on his way to the other cruiser. After a brief conversation with the first officer, Tommy approached Michael's car. The other cruiser drove off.

Michael rolled down his window. Tommy stood tall, arms folded across his chest.

"You're making this too easy, Riordan." He wore a smug grin. "Get out of the car."

Alone on a country road with Phillip Morgan's enforcer. How did he let this happen? Getting out of the car would be a bad idea.

"I think I should stay right where I am, thank you."

Tommy shook his head. "I must not have heard you correctly, because I thought you just refused a direct request from a police officer."

"There's nothing wrong with your ears," Michael continued under his breath, "Can't say the same for what's between them."

Tommy rested his hand on his gun. "Did you say something, Riordan?"

"Am I under arrest?"

"Not yet." He flashed a twisted smile. "Have you been drinking?"

"No."

"The other officer seemed to think so."

"I had a soda at lunch. Dr. Pepper. You can ask the waitress. I think her name was Kate."

Tommy unbuttoned his pocket and pulled out a Breathalyzer. "You're going to have to step out of the car for a sobriety test."

"I told you I haven't had any alcohol."

"I'm just doing my job." He stepped aside. "Now, get out of the car."

Michael held up one hand. "Fine!" He reached into his pocket with his other hand and engaged the voice recorder app on his phone.

Michael blew into the small device, and Tommy studied it.

"How'd I do?"

Tommy grinned. "I'm afraid I'm going to have to arrest you for DWI. Says so right here."

"Not possible."

Tommy pushed him up against the car. "Anything's possible out here."

"This is harassment, and you know it."

"Looks like it's your word against mine, Mr. Wiseass." Tommy showed his teeth. "You best mind your manners, or I'll add resisting arrest to the charges."

"You're not going to get away with it this time."

"Who's gonna stop me?"

Michael pulled his phone from his pocket. He tapped the screen a couple of times and their conversation played from the speaker. *Anything's possible out here... This is harassment, and you know it... Looks like it's your word against mine, Mr. Wiseass... You best mind your manners, or I'll add resisting arrest to the charges. You're not gonna get away with it this time. Who's gonna stop me?*

He slipped his phone back in his pocket before Tommy got any ideas about grabbing it. A car approached. Tommy watched it drive by. Another followed close behind.

Tommy turned to Michael, neck muscles tight and nostrils flared. "Get back in the car."

Michael was eager to comply.

"Stay put." He turned and marched in the direction of his car.

Tommy sat in his cruiser for what seemed like an hour. He returned and held out Michael's license and registration wrapped in a traffic citation. He pulled it back when Michael reached for it.

"I told you to get that tail light fixed." A smug smile flickered across his lips. "Maybe next time you'll listen to me."

Tommy tossed the papers through the window into Michael's lap. "This is your third strike, Riordan. You don't get any more."

Tommy walked back to his cruiser, placed his hand on the door handle, and turned. He stared at Michael who watched through the windshield, then flashed the *I'm watching you* sign with his free hand.

Later that night, Michael reclined in a chair by the pool, a bottle of beer on the table next to him. The full moon illuminated the yard with an eerie silver light. The vendetta Tommy had against him had gotten out of hand, and he thought about how he might neutralize the threat that he now posed.

On the bright side, his writing seemed to benefit from all the recent drama. He'd spent most of the afternoon in his office at his laptop, then reviewed his work outside by the pool until it became too dark to see. He set the manuscript down and took another pull on the beer.

His thoughts turned again to Emily. She was stubborn, always had been. But this predicament he was in was his fault. He'd let her down, pushed her away with his own misguided stubbornness.

Michael closed his eyes and remembered the times he—or more precisely, Richard—had criticized her stubbornness, which she called determination. I'm not stubborn, she'd say. My way is just better. Admittedly, more often than not, she was right. Like her constant suggestions that they spend more time together—an impromptu day trip, or perhaps just an afternoon in the park or by the lake. In his mind, there were always more pressing matters, too much work to be done. But Emily never let up, never stopped trying. Until she did. He wore her down, broken her spirit. The roses that he wouldn't stop to smell were trampled underfoot.

"Michael!"

His eyes snapped opened, and he turned toward the voice. "Hey, Ang." He let out a long breath. "How are you?"

She stopped dead in her tracks and pointed at the bottle. "What the hell is that?"

Michael glanced at it and then back at his sister.

"Dammit, Michael!"

He gestured toward an empty chair. "Please, Ang, just sit down."

She didn't move.

He'd had a trying day with his father, then Tommy. Now this? He decided to man-up and do something about it.

"I insist." He pointed to the empty chair. "We need to talk."

CHAPTER **THIRTY-ONE**

Angie reached for the bottle and picked it up between her thumb and forefinger, holding it away from her body as if it contained toxic waste. "Not with this thing here." In one fluid motion, she heaved it into the yard.

Michael sighed.

Angela set her keys on the table and leaned back in her chair. "So, what is it you wanted to talk about?"

He hesitated. "Remember the day you broke into my house and—"

"I have a key, Michael," she reminded him, and folded her arms across her chest.

"Okay, but remember when you asked me who I thought was in the house?"

He waited for a response but had to settle for her impatient glare.

"I thought it might be Emily's brother, Tommy."

"Tommy?" She tilted her head and scrunched her nose. "Why would—"

"He threatened me the night of the wedding. He's working for Phillip Morgan and he warned me to stay away from Emily."

Her eyes grew wide. "Seriously? What are you going to do?"

"Do?" he said a little too loudly. He lowered his voice. "Nothing. He's a cop."

"You've got to at least tell her, Michael."

"But he's her brother. And it's not the first time he's done something like this," he said, opening the door to the real reason for their conversation.

"How do you know that?"

"Because he did it to me once before. Twenty-five years ago."

Angie stared, slackjawed. "How is that even possible?"

"I'm not who I appear to be."

"You've been acting pretty strange since the accident, but I just figured—"

"Yeah, you figured I got my bell rung a little too hard and needed some time to recover." He paused. "It's a little more complicated than that."

"What do you mean?"

"I mean your brother died in that accident."

She let out a nervous laugh. "Come on, Michael, you're creeping me out."

"I'm sorry, Angie, but I need your help. I can't do this alone anymore. I have to tell someone."

"Tell someone what?"

A dog barked in the yard next door. Michael glanced toward the sound.

"What is it, Michael?"

He leaned closer. "Do you know what a walk-in is?"

Her eyes narrowed. "You mean like when you don't have an appointment?"

He shook his head. "More like... *Heaven Can Wait*."

"The movie?"

Michael nodded. "After Warren Beatty dies, his soul comes back and trades places with another. He's given the chance to continue his life in the body of someone else." He took a deep breath. "Michael is my someone else."

"Are you drunk?" she snorted. "God, Michael. What the hell is wrong with you?"

Their eyes locked. Michael remained silent.

"That's impossible." Angela stood. "If that were true, then who were... I mean are... *Shit!* I don't know what I mean."

"My name was Richard Dunham."

Angie blinked, as if unsure she'd heard him correctly. "You mean the jerk who caused your accident?"

"I wouldn't have put it that way, but yes." He studied her reaction.

"This is crazy, Michael. Stop it." She walked over to the edge of the pool, presumably to put some distance between them. "How many beers have you had tonight?"

Michael didn't answer.

She turned to face him. "I don't believe any of this."

"I know it sounds crazy, but it's true. Why would I make something like this up?"

A silence stretched out between them.

"You said it yourself. I've been acting strange since the accident. Now you know why."

She turned away and stared into the water. "And Michael?"

"I'm sorry, Ang, but he's gone." He stood and walked to her side. In the moonlight, her expression was unreadable. "I would have told you sooner, but I didn't know how."

Tears fell, and she wiped them several times before looking at him. "I guess that would explain some things... like forgetting you're an alcoholic. People don't forget things like that."

"I don't imagine they do. I did lose my memory for a while. All of it. I didn't know who I was, where I was, or how I got there until Richard's memories began to come back."

She closed her eyes. He waited. "So, what's this have to do with Emily's brother?" she asked.

"Emily is my wife."

Her eyes widened. "You've got to be kidding."

"I wish I was." He paused. "I wish this was all some big joke, and I could go back to the way things were before I... before the accident."

"You have to stop talking like this or they'll put you back in the hospital." Her tears glistened in the moonlight.

"I hoped you'd understand." He touched her arm just above the elbow. "I need an ally; someone I can talk to. Someone I can be honest with."

"Honest?" She pulled her arm away and let the word hang there for a moment.

"Look, I understand this is difficult, but please don't shut me out. It's a lot to process, so just—"

She walked back to the table and picked up her keys. "I have to go."

"Angie..."

"You need professional help."

Michael grabbed her arm.

Angie pulled it away. "Don't touch me."

"OK. No more touching." Michael held up his hands. "But I need to show you something before you go."

"I'm really not in the mood."

"Humor me," Michael said.

Angie followed him into the house and waited in the kitchen. He disappeared into the living room. She crossed her arms and waited for Michael to return. When he didn't, she turned to go. "I'm leaving."

Music floated in from the living room, and she stopped in her tracks. She listened for a moment before walking slowly toward the sound. Michael continued to play a complicated piece on the piano while she watched from the doorway.

"Stop it," she shouted.

Michael obliged. "You don't like it?"

"There's no way you just played that."

"So, you agree there's something weird going on here? That I might be telling the truth?"

He waited for her response, which didn't come.

After a vacant stare, Angie made a dash for the back door.

CHAPTER **THIRTY-TWO**

For the next few days, Angie was M.I.A. Michael suddenly missed her showing up unannounced, eating his food, and offering her near-sighted opinions and off-color remarks. She was the closest thing he had to an ally, and he second-guessed his ill-fated attempt at honesty, which may have driven her away for good.

Michael knocked on the door of the guest house and waited. He wasn't at all sure what he'd say to smooth things over. It's not every day that you find out your only brother has died and someone else has commandeered his body. It wouldn't be easy, but he needed to keep the lines of communication open.

He knocked again, then cupped his hands and peered through the glass into an empty room. A few of Angie's things were visible inside so, apparently, she hadn't slipped out of town in the middle of the night. He lingered a few moments until he was convinced no one was home.

Angie pulled herself up until her eyes cleared the kitchen counter and stared at the door for a moment to make sure Michael had gone. She crept to the window and watched through the blinds as Michael disappeared inside the main house.

She dropped down on the sofa and rested her head on one of the throw pillows. Clearly, Michael was getting worse instead of better. At first, it had been easy to blame some of

Michael's strange behavior and missing memories on the accident. But after his confession a few days ago, she was convinced that he'd spun out of control. Or perhaps this was all an elaborate charade designed to make her look like a fool. Her logical mind told her it had to be. But why? Why would Michael do something like that?

The man had a lot of nerve, she thought. Even if his appearance at her door had been to come clean and deliver an apology, she wasn't ready to talk to him, much less forgive him.

One thing troubled her more than all the others. How did he play that damn piano? How could he possibly have pulled that one off?

Michael sat on his sofa, disheveled, and stared at his laptop. Angie hadn't showed her face for over a week. He'd thrown himself into his writing. Long hours at his laptop, alternating between Red Bull and Heineken. Pizza and Chinese take-out filled the hole in his stomach but had little effect on the void in his heart.

The doorbell rang and Michael opened it to find Angie on his porch.

"You look like hell," she said, her disappointment tempered by concern.

Michael stood aside and closed the door behind Angie. "What are you doing here? Have a change of heart?"

Angie stepped over debris as she walked into the room. "I didn't say that."

"Then, what do you want?"

"I needed some space after your big announcement. But I haven't heard from you in almost two weeks."

"You're the one who went off the grid. I've been right here."

"I was... worried... alright?"

"Well, don't be. I'm fine."

The room looked like a bomb went off. Angie surveyed the damage. "I can see that."

An awkward silence followed.

"How did you play the piano like that?" Angie asked.

"Years of lessons."

"You never took lessons."

"Michael didn't."

Angie folded her arms across her chest. "So that's your story and you're sticking to it?"

"I have a surprise," Michael said with the first smile of the day. "I've been writing. Turns out I can do that, too."

"I hope this means you're—"

"I'm finished."

Angie glanced at Michael's laptop on the coffee table, surrounded by empty beer bottles and pizza boxes. She shook her head. "Finished acting like a drunken hermit, I hope."

Michael cleared off the sofa, took a seat, and patted the cushion. Reluctantly, Angie sat next to him.

"It's been... therapeutic'" he said.

"Really? How does it end?"

"Did I say I was finished? I meant *almost* finished. It needs an ending."

Angie shook her head again, something she'd done a lot lately. "You'll be in deep shit if you don't give whatever you have to Rhonda, ASAP."

"I needed to write it." Michael sighed. "I'm not sure I want anyone to read it."

"What about me? I'm not just anyone... Am I?"

Michael hesitated, then picked up an empty pizza box from the coffee table to expose a stack of printed paper held together with a binder clip. "Read it if you like, just get it out of my sight. I'm not sure what I'm going to do with it, but right now, I don't want it here."

Angie picked it up and scooted over to the end of the sofa. "By the way, you really need a shower."

Michael hesitated, then spoke in a flat voice. "I had a sister."

Angie rolled her eyes. "You still do."

"Her name was Julie."

Angie glared.

"We hadn't spoken in years."

"I'm not surprised." Her eyes avoided his. "What kind of twisted shit did you dump on *her*?"

Michael floated across the pool on an inflatable raft, the afternoon sun warm on his back. He drifted in and out of an alcohol-induced sleep, his mind comfortably numb. The corner of the raft kissed the bull-nosed tile along the edge of the pool and gently reversed direction. Seconds later, fear and confusion shattered his silent reverie. Water filled his nose and mouth. His eyes opened to the burn of chlorine.

Michael flailed around for a moment before his feet touched the bottom of the pool. He fought to regain his balance as the burn spread to his lungs. He stood, pushed his hair back, and blinked away the pain. He heaved with a ragged cough.

Angie stood, arms folded, and watched him from the edge of the pool.

"What'd you do that for?" Tiny drops of water sprayed from his mouth when he spoke.

She glared for a moment, shook her head, and walked away.

CHAPTER **THIRTY-THREE**

Michael stood in the kitchen, towel around his waist, making a sandwich when the doorbell rang. He set the mayo jar down and walked into the living room.

Carl Dunham smiled when Michael opened the door.

Michael stuck his head outside, looked left and right, then pulled his father inside. "What are you doing here?"

"So, this is where you live? Not bad."

"I'd give you a tour, but you're leaving."

Carl walked to the sofa and sat. "Things are different now. What do you say we bury the hatchet?"

"You've already done that. In my back."

"C'mon, Son. Forever's a long time to stay mad."

Michael folded his arms across his chest. "Years ago, you couldn't wait to leave. Now, I can't seem to get rid of you."

"It's all about perspective."

The doorbell rang. Michael looked at Carl like he might know who it was. Carl shrugged. Michael took a few steps toward the door, then froze when the banging started.

"I know you're in there, Michael," Rhonda called from the other side of the door.

Carl smiled. "Your car's in the driveway."

"Shhhh."

Rhonda banged the door harder, and Michael winced. He turned toward Carl with a finger to his lips. They waited silently until she left.

"Sounds like you've got a whole new set of problems, Dorothy."

Michael glared. "You need to leave."

"What if she sees me?"

"Use the back door."

"Why won't you let me help you?"

"You've done enough."

"I can see you've got everything under control."

"Don't let the door hit you on the way out."

"Tick tock, Son."

Lexi set two cups of tea on the table and sat across from her mother.

"Thank you for letting me camp out here while they work on my kitchen." Emily hung her purse on the back of the chair and sat.

"Are you kidding me? I made the mistake of telling Kayla last week that Gramma was going to stay with us for a while. She hasn't stopped talking about it."

Emily stirred in some honey and stared into her cup.

"Mom?" Lexi leaned in closer. "Is everything okay?"

"I don't know." Emily sipped her tea.

Lexi's eyes held a measure of concern.

"A man kissed me," Emily said after an awkward pause.

"I just assumed you and Phillip were—"

"It wasn't Phillip."

"Who was it?"

"His name's Michael Riordan."

"The writer?" Lexi set down her cup. "So, you only date celebrities now?"

"I'm not dating anyone."

"Sounds like you've got a choice to make."

Emily wrinkled her brow. "Phillip is way too controlling... but there's something weird about Michael."

"Weird?"

"He reminds me of your father, which is definitely not what I need right now."

Lexi relaxed. "I hope you wouldn't dismiss someone just because they remind you of Dad. He wasn't a bad man."

"I don't feel like debating this again, Lex."

"Good. Neither do I. I'm just saying that's no reason to avoid someone you like."

"I don't like him."

"Your eyes tell me otherwise."

Michael grabbed the bottle of Scotch that he'd stashed behind the cereal boxes to hide from Angela's judgmental eyes. She still had a problem with him having a drink now and then. She didn't understand. He set it down on the counter and shook his head. He'd become one of those sorry souls who hid booze around the house. Perhaps Angie was right.

Michael sat down with the bottle in his favorite chair in the living room. He picked up an empty glass that had been left on the end table and blew into it. Clean enough. He poured himself a drink, opened his laptop, and read the words he'd written over the past two weeks.

He searched for answers from his past, but grew more distracted with each whiff of the smoky liquid in his glass. It had an earthy quality, like wet leaves burning, or perhaps a smoldering campfire. It stirred up unfamiliar memories. Vague recollections of someone else's life became intertwined with his own thoughts.

As the evening wore on, Michael lost count of how many times he refilled his glass. It's a small glass, he told himself. His frustration grew with every word he read. Memories that didn't belong clamored for his attention. Finally, he'd had enough and closed the laptop. He set it on the hearth, picked up his half-full glass, and paced around the room.

He tried to dismiss the idea that the real Michael Riordan had somehow returned in an attempt to regain control. He didn't recall Arthur ever mentioning such a scenario. Could he be running out of time? Or did the physical body somehow retain fragments of Michael's past in its DNA?

His eyes were drawn to the large, gold-handled sword that hung above the fireplace. He stared at it for a moment before releasing it from its mount. Heavy and unwieldy, he held it in front of him with both hands like a warrior.

Emily's voice echoed in his head—words that haunted him. *What happened to my romantic warrior?*

Michael moved about the room with purpose. He swung the sword in an imaginary battle. He stopped to catch his breath before he let out a battle cry and brought the sword down hard, nearly cutting his laptop in half.

His hands shook from the post-adrenaline crash. He returned the sword to the wall with the sinking feeling that he hadn't yet killed the beast. He slumped back into his chair, spent from the battle. He closed his eyes to rest. When he opened them, he noticed movement by the fireplace and squinted to get a better look. The words—his words—rose in bizarre animation from the broken machine. They moved slowly at first but gained momentum as they climbed. He rubbed his eyes.

Soon, thousands of them formed a cloud that spun like a tornado, a whirling dervish with arms that reached for him, and tried to pull him in. The beast would consume him, judging him for the sins of his past. He couldn't let that happen. He squeezed his eyes shut for a moment. When he opened them, the beast was gone.

His story had become a living, breathing thing—a monster he had resurrected, word by word, cloaked in emotion. It was the story of his life, a life that had somehow spun out of control. He could have stopped it, but he didn't. Arthur had told him life was about choices, and he continued to make them, each one worse than the last. It had to stop.

A small amount of liquid remained in the bottom of his glass, and he knocked it to the floor with the back of his hand. He pulled himself up from his seat, walked over to the fireplace, and picked up the pieces of his laptop. With what was left of the beast tucked under his arm, he grabbed his keys and left the house in a hurry.

CHAPTER **THIRTY-FOUR**

Michael leaned against the Overlook railing, and watched the ripples spread across the surface of the water. One after another, they moved silently toward shore, and faded helplessly before they reached their destination. A sense of desolation and disillusionment overwhelmed him, and he turned to leave. Michael disappeared down the east trail toward the parking lot.

Emily reached the top of the west trail and stepped onto the empty platform. The black water looked as smooth as glass below. She leaned against the rail and whispered into the night.

"I thought we had a deal, Richard. Whoever died first would send messages from the other side." She shook her head. "I guess that was a lie, too."

Emily waited for a few minutes, eyes closed. "That's it? You've got nothing to say for yourself?" Her back stiffened. "You'd better not be sending messages to *her*."

She didn't stay long. In fact, she wasn't sure why she'd come to a place so crowded with memories. She walked sluggishly down the trail to the parking lot, fear tightening its stranglehold on her heart. Her life had changed unexpectedly, her world turned upside down. Fear of the unknown nearly paralyzed her.

Twilight had given way to night. Emily used the small solar lights that lined the edges of the trail to make her way back, thankful that she'd parked under one of the three lamps that cast funnels of light on the pavement. She jogged the last fifty feet, unlocked her car, and slipped inside. She turned the key in the ignition and stared out through the windshield at a small piece of paper that someone had tucked under her wiper blade.

Hesitant to leave the relative safety of her car, she rolled down her window and snatched the paper. She read the words written in a familiar hand. *Give Michael another chance.* Her brow furrowed.

She scanned the empty parking lot from her driver's seat, then sped off into the night.

Michael struggled with an unrelenting stream of memories on the drive home. He could drive his car off the nearest bridge, but a fatal accident is what had landed him in this place, this alternate reality. Where might he end up if it happened again? How much worse might it be if his early demise was self-inflicted?

Michael unlocked the door and stepped into his dark living room. He flipped the light switch and stopped in his tracks. Angie watched him from the sofa.

"Jeezus, Ang."

Angie didn't move except to hook a thumb in the direction of the fireplace where pieces of the laptop still remained. "What happened over there?"

Michael dropped his keys on the small table by the door. "I had a little trouble with my laptop," he said in a flat voice.

"Where is it now?"

"Franklin Park."

Angie tilted her head. "I don't understand."

He didn't need her to understand. His relief at seeing her again after her disappearing act was tempered by her need to meddle in every detail of his life. "Let's just say it made a bigger splash than I expected."

"Michael!" Angie stood. "What about your book? You have a backup, right?"

"Of course." He wished she would disappear again. "It's on a flash drive."

Angie relaxed and returned to her seat on the sofa

"That splash wasn't nearly as big."

"What the hell is wrong with you?" Angie, on her feet again, studied him. "You're drunk."

"We're not going to do this again, are we?"

"You need to come to a meeting."

Michael picked up his keys and turned around.

"You can't outrun this."

He opened the door to leave.

"I came here to tell you how good your story is. Believe me, I didn't want to like it."

Michael stopped, his hand on the doorknob. "What's the point?"

"I can help you."

Michael turned. "I told you. I'm not an alcoholic."

"We can do it together."

"You don't understand. I'm running out of time."

"It's never too late. You did it once before, you can do it again."

Michael frowned and set his keys back on the table. He looked at Angie curiously. "Do what again?"

Angie tossed him his sobriety coin. "I found it in the trash."

Michael set it on the table next to his keys. "This isn't the problem. It's Emily."

"Fine. Then do it for her."

Michael said nothing.

"You think she wants..." She gestured toward Michael. "This?!!"

"I said, I don't want to talk about it."

"Don't be such a pussy."

Michael shifted his weight and shot her a hard glare.

"Wake up, Michael. When you're the best you can be, you allow her to do the same."

"She's not coming around like I'd hoped."

"If opportunity doesn't knock, you might need to build a door."

Michael shoved his hands in his pockets and relaxed a bit. "I kissed her."

Angie's hard expression softened a bit. "Now we're getting somewhere. Did she kiss you back?" She flashed a tell-me-more smile.

"Sort of." They both sat on the sofa. "Just before she ran away."

"Maybe you need to work on your kissing skills."

"Funny, Ang. She said we were done. I think she felt the same thing I did, and it scared her."

"I don't know what to believe anymore." Angie awkwardly placed an arm around Michael's shoulder and gave him a squeeze. "You need to come with me to a meeting, Bro."

Michael stood quickly. "I'm NOT an alcoholic."

"Clearly." Angie rolled her eyes. "Maybe you need to tell Emily the truth."

"Look how well that worked with you."

"I'm still here." She smiled briefly before her expression became serious. "You need to let me help you."

"I wish you could."

Angie hesitated. "I gave your manuscript to Rhonda."

"You did *what?*"

"You can thank me later."

"That's not funny..." He waited for her to admit that she wasn't serious. When she didn't, "You're kidding, right?"

"It's time to put on your big-boy pants and start acting like—"

"I thought you wanted to help me."

"I'm trying. Are you?"

"You need to go."

"You need to man-up and tell her."

CHAPTER **THIRTY-FIVE**

The next morning, Michael flipped the lid open on one of the trash bins in the garage. He deposited two large garbage bags and three empty pizza boxes inside and slammed the lid. Angie was right about one thing. He needed to tell Emily. This was a new day. He'd wallowed his last wallow. He brushed off his hands and walked outside. Time to make a move and deal with the consequences. He dropped into one of the chairs by the pool and pulled out his phone.

"Emily. I need to see you. I have something important to tell you... No. Not over the phone... Please... You need to hear this... Fine. I'll pick you up at eight."

Michael set the phone on the small glass table next to his chair, leaned back, and closed his eyes. A small weight had been lifted from his shoulders. The heavy one wouldn't be shed until Emily knew the truth.

A ball bounced on the basketball court, and he opened his eyes. He wasn't sure how long they'd been closed.

"Hey!"

Michael turned.

Carl Dunham stood at center court. "You up for a little one-on-one?"

Michael shook his head. "You're not going to leave me alone, are you?" He walked toward the court.

"I did that once. We both know how that turned out."

Michael stopped a few feet away. "You never wanted to play when I was a kid. Why start now?"

Carl passed him the ball. "Why not?"

"Nothing I ever did was good enough."

"So, what did you do about it?"

"At some point, I guess I just stopped trying."

"Is that what you did with Emily?"

"No!" Michael hesitated. "Maybe."

Carl smiled. "Your best is always good enough."

Michael fired the ball back and took a defensive position. "You're up first, old man."

Carl made a quick move to the basket, but was rejected. The two men traded baskets, and the competition heated up. Michael went hard to the hoop and knocked his father to the ground.

Carl looked up. "How did that feel?"

"Not as good as I'd hoped."

"I'll admit, I've never been a strong player."

Michael offered a hand and pulled him up. "Don't you mean father?"

"I tried, Richard."

"You should have tried harder. I was twelve when you left us to fend for ourselves."

"I made a mistake. Things didn't exactly work out the way I planned." Carl's expression softened. He tilted his head. "Haven't you ever made a mistake?"

Michael ignored the question. "Why didn't you come back home?"

"I wanted to. But I didn't think that was an option. I took the easy way out."

"Easy for who?"

"Exactly."

Michael bit down on his lower lip. He shifted the ball from one hand to the other. "So, why are you here?"

"To help you, Son."

"I don't need your help, Carl. You're too late."

"Would it kill you to call me Dad?"

"Like I said, I don't need your help, Carl."

He took the ball from Michael and dribbled a couple times before looking up. "The past here is not always the same past there."

Michael reached for the ball, but Carl pulled it away. "How can I have more than one past? I don't remember any others."

"That's because your consciousness can only be in one place at a time."

"How can I be there—or anywhere—if I'm here?"

"You're there. You're just not aware of it."

"My brain hurts."

"After your accident, your consciousness moved from there to here."

"But before the accident, here was there and there was here?"

"You're smarter than you look. There becomes here when your consciousness moves."

"Is that what happens when you die?"

"Yes and no." Carl dribbled the ball a couple times.

"My brain hurts again."

"It's true that your consciousness moves when you die. But you don't necessarily come here. Where you go is a choice."

"So, you're saying I chose this?"

"Perhaps not consciously."

"Why? Why here? And why are you still you, and I'm someone else?"

Carl tucked the ball under his arm and met Michael's gaze. "You needed a different perspective."

"And you didn't?"

"Everyone's situation is different."

Michael said nothing.

"Emily needed to be the object of Richard's emotional and physical attention."

"I guess I could've been more... *attentive.*"

"Imagine how she felt when she believed that the attention she craved was given to another woman?"

"But—"

"Imagine."

"Fine. I imagine it felt the way I do now when I see her with Phillip."

"Emily's not married. She's done nothing wrong. She's not broken any vow."

"You made your point." He wrinkled his brow. "So, what happened *here?* In the past?"

"Emily thinks you had an affair. I'm afraid it's the same here as it was there."

"Did I?"

"What do you think?"

"I would never do that."

"Then, that's all you need to know."

"Says you."

"The past is past. It's what we do next that matters."

Michael wished his old man had shared some of this wisdom with him sooner. "Why didn't you tell me all this the first time we met?"

"Would you have listened?"

The answer was probably no. "It still doesn't explain why I turned into this Michael character."

"Like I said, you needed a different perspective." Carl nodded like he had all the answers. "You're on the outside looking in now. Much easier to be objective."

"What about Arthur?"

A smile flickered on Carl's face. "That was me."

"What do you mean?"

"Your dead father couldn't just pop back into his old timeline." He shrugged. "Would you have believed anything I said if I showed up at the shelter like this?"

A few seconds passed. Michael frowned. "By the way… an alcoholic? That's the best you could do?"

Carl flashed a twisted smile. "It's the best I could do on short notice." He launched a shot toward the other end of the court.

Michael watched the ball arc toward the basket and slip through the net with a *swish*. He turned, eyes wide, but his father was gone.

CHAPTER **THIRTY-SIX**

Michael stood on Lexi's front porch. Emily had asked that he pick her up at her daughter's house. Apparently, she'd been staying there during her kitchen renovation. He wondered if she'd be jetting off to Ireland any time soon.

Emily had sounded surprised when he called. It had been nearly two weeks since their lunch in Riverside, and he couldn't tell if she expected to hear from him sooner or never again. He told her he had something important to discuss, regardless of which way their relationship was headed.

Michael reached for the doorknob, then stopped halfway. In another time—and another body—he would have walked right in. He didn't know what to expect when he came face to face with his daughter, let alone his little granddaughter. He could barely hold it together just thinking about it. There would be no hugs and kisses for this virtual stranger.

He rang the bell and waited on the front porch. Emily smiled politely and let him in. He remembered the weekends he'd spent helping Lexi and her husband refurbish the hundred-year-old Victorian home. Emily had been by his side much of the time. He recalled the paintbrush fight they'd had the day Lexi left them alone to paint the dining room. At least one of the window frames still held telltale signs of their playful skirmish.

Their eyes met for only a moment before Lexi appeared from the living room.

"Alexis, this is my friend, Michael." She gestured toward Lexi. "My daughter, Alexis."

"Nice to meet you." Michael studied his daughter, and his heart turned a somersault.

Lexi smiled politely.

"That's Kayla," Emily continued. She pointed to the living room.

Michael glanced in her direction, then back to Emily, who appeared in good spirits. Had she loosened up a bit, or was it an Oscar-worthy performance?

"I just need a few minutes with Lexi before we leave," Emily said.

"Take your time."

Michael stood in the foyer while Emily followed Lexi into the kitchen. He peeked into the living room where Kayla watched television.

"Hello," he said.

Her little face lit up. "Hi, Grampa." She ran toward him.

Michael shot a quick glance toward the kitchen to see if anyone had overheard them. When Kayla reached him, he squatted down and held out his hand, afraid of how a big hug might appear to the women if they happened to walk in.

"Hello, Lady Bug." He shook her small hand.

"Let's go play," she said.

He stood and held out his finger like Grampa used to. Kayla wrapped her hand around it and pulled him toward the corner of the living room. He turned his head to see Emily watching from the kitchen, a strange look on her face. He shrugged.

Emily stared for a moment before she turned back to Lexi.

"Sit down, Grampa," Kayla said when they reached the appropriate spot.

He obliged after he shot another glance in the direction of the kitchen. He sat cross-legged on the floor, intrigued by the fact that she had called him "Grampa."

"Do you remember who I am?"

She looked at him like he was the child. "Grampa, of course."

His knee ached and he shifted his weight.

"How come you didn't come over for a long time?" she asked.

He cleared his throat. "It's not because I didn't want to, Sweetie. I had to go away for a while."

"To heaven?"

He hesitated with an answer.

"Gramma said you went to heaven."

"Well, we know that Grammas are always right, don't we?"

"Yup."

"Time's up," Emily called from the dining room.

"Be right there." He turned back to Kayla. "Grampa has to go now."

"Bye," she said, busy mixing up something on her little stove.

"I'd like to come back and play again sometime."

"Okay."

Michael stood up slowly and watched Kayla for a moment before he left the room. The two women met him in the hall.

Lexi walked into the living room. "Put your things away, honey. It's time for bed."

Emily studied Michael, then gave a nod. "We'd better go."

Outside, she asked, "So, where are you taking me?"

"I figured we'd go to Winslow's. We can get a booth in the back where no one will see us."

She watched him as he held the car door open. "There's something we need to talk about?"

"Let's wait until we get there."

"I don't like surprises, Michael." She twirled a lock of hair around her finger.

"I know," he said. "Just promise to keep an open mind."

"Like that's supposed to make me feel better?"

Michael felt her stare as he started the car. He kept his eyes on the rearview mirror and backed out of the driveway.

CHAPTER **THIRTY-SEVEN**

Tommy McKenna climbed the porch steps, the soft crunch of leather from his uniform echoing his progress. He pressed the doorbell and waited with his arms folded across his chest.

"Hi, Uncle Tommy," Lexi said when she opened the door, clearly surprised by his impromptu visit.

"Hey, Lex. Can I come in?"

"Sure." She stepped aside and let him pass.

Tommy looked around the room for a moment. He didn't get to see much of his niece or her family. Their visits were usually limited to the Fourth of July, Christmas, and perhaps the occasional meeting at her grandparents' house. He sensed her apprehension.

"What are you doing here?" she asked politely.

"I understand that your mom's been staying with you."

"She's having some work done at her house, so she'll be here for a few days."

"That's real nice of you." He smiled. "Is she here now?"

"No, she went out."

"Hmmm... maybe you can help me." He unbuttoned his shirt pocket, pulled out a photograph, and handed it to her. "Have you seen this man?"

Lexi studied it for only a second or two before looking up at him with wide eyes. "His name is Michael. He was just here."

Tommy retrieved the photo and slipped it back into his pocket. "How long ago?"

"About ten minutes. He picked Mom up and they left."

"Know where they went?"

She shook her head, then cleared her throat. "Is she in some kind of danger?"

Tommy put his hand on her shoulder. "She'll be fine." He put his burly arms around her and gave her a hug. "Your Uncle Tommy would never let anything bad happen to his little sister. You know that."

Lexi nodded.

"Are you sure she didn't say anything about where they were going?" He released her and took a step backward.

"I think they went out for a drink. She said she wouldn't be late."

"That's good, Lex. Thanks."

"She's known him for a while," she added. "I've heard his name before, but this is the first time I met him."

"He's not a criminal or anything like that," Tommy assured her. *At least as far as I can tell at the moment.* "I just want to talk to him."

Lexi relaxed a bit. "What should I tell her when she gets back?"

"Nothing." His expression became serious. "You have to promise me you won't say anything to her about our little talk tonight."

"Why?"

"I know your mom. No sense getting her all worked up over nothing."

"But—"

"Please, Lex. It's important. You need to trust me."

She had no reason not to. Lexi smiled an uneasy smile. "Okay."

Tommy reassured her she had no need to worry. "Kayla in bed?"

"I just put her down a few minutes ago."

"Well, you tell her I said hey."

Lexi nodded.

Tommy hit redial on his cell phone when he reached the sidewalk.

"They're out together," he said into the phone. "About fifteen minutes ago. I don't know, but it sounds like they went to a bar..." The call ended abruptly. Tommy stared at his phone, then shook his head. He pocketed the phone and slid into the driver's seat of the police cruiser.

After a moment, he slammed his hands on the steering wheel.

Michael chose a booth in the back corner at Winslow's. He hoped a little alcohol might soften the blow. He ordered two glasses of wine. *In vino veritas.* No smoky memories, just the truth.

They chatted for a short time, mostly small talk, until Emily had nearly finished her first drink. Michael ordered her another.

"Well?" Her eyes searched his.

Michael had been stalling, unsure how or where to begin.

"I thought you had something to tell me," she said. "Isn't that why we're here?"

"Yes, of course." He wiped his hands on his thighs. "It's just that... okay, you have to remember that I would never lie to you, Emily."

"Just say it, Michael." She picked up her glass.

"Don't you think it was a little odd that I knew your dog's name and your favorite wine?" He pointed to her glass as she set it down. "Our conversations have been so easy, and we seem to have so much in common, like we've known each other forever. Have you noticed?"

She pushed away from the table, as if the extra few inches between them offered some additional protection. "Have you been stalking me? Please tell me you're not some psycho serial killer." Her eyes, laced with fear, darted around the room.

"Absolutely not," he assured her. "But we've known each other much longer than you might think."

"What do you mean? How?"

He had an idea. "Do you remember the show *The Ghost Whisperer?*"

She tilted her head. "Sure, but what does that—?"

"Do you believe the things that happened on the show are possible?"

"I suppose so," she said slowly. "I guess if I didn't, I wouldn't have watched it."

"Good point. Do you remember when Melinda's husband Jim died?"

"Yes." She frowned.

"Okay. Do you remember the episode shortly after that where Jim's spirit didn't want to leave Melinda, so he walked into Sam's body right after a car accident?"

"Yes, Melinda was upset. She wanted him to move on."

"Okay, not so much that part. I'm talking about the whole walk-in thing." He paused to take a drink. "Do you think that sort of thing ever happens... I mean, in real life?"

"Well," she hesitated, "I don't know anyone who's done it, but I guess it's possible."

He took another drink. "What if you did? Know someone, that is."

"Michael, I'm sure you didn't bring me here to discuss a TV show. What's going on?"

How do I do this? How do tell her I'm really the soul of her dead husband who just happens to have taken up residence in another man's body? And how do I explain waiting this long to tell her?

"Michael?"

No answer.

"Earth to Michael..."

"Hmmm?" His head gave a little jerk and his eyes met hers.

"Where were you? We were talking and you just left, zoned right out. What's the matter with you? Why are we here?"

"I'm sorry, I just—"

Emily's phone rang and Michael stopped talking. He welcomed the momentary interruption.

She pulled the phone from her purse and stared at the screen. "I'm sorry," she said when it rang again. "I should take this."

Michael nodded.

"Hello," she said into her phone. "What? No, I don't remember."

Michael watched her.

Her eyes met his. "You're kidding." She looked away and lowered her voice. "But I'm not dressed for... okay, fine." She slipped the phone back into her purse and took a big gulp of wine.

"Is everything ok?"

"No. I have to go." She seemed mildly annoyed.

"Now?" he asked a little too loudly and heads turned. He glanced around the room then back to Emily. "Please don't leave," he said calmly. "I'm not finished."

"I'm sorry, Michael."

"At least let me drive you home."

"Phillip's out front."

Michael blinked. "What?"

"I know, right?" She twirled her hair around her finger.

"How did he know where you were?"

"He just does." She sighed and stood.

Michael looked up, confused.

"I'm sorry."

Michael forced a smile and watched her walk away.

Every eye in the room rested on him while he sat alone in the empty booth. He replayed the conversation in his head and his frustration grew—frustration with himself for not being able to tell her the truth and frustration with Prince Freakin' Phillip who seemed to have Emily Dunham wrapped around his gold-plated, little finger.

Michael slammed his fist on the table. Heads turned again. A waitress approached, but he continued to stare at the empty seat where Emily sat only a moment ago.

"Excuse me." The waitress pointed to his glass. "Can I get you another?"

"I'm sorry, what?"

"Would you like another drink?" she asked.

It's hard enough to keep from walking over to the bar, but when the bar walks over to you...

"I can come back," she said and turned to leave.

"I'll have a Scotch. Neat."

She picked up the empty glass and walked away.

CHAPTER **THIRTY-EIGHT**

Mentally, Richard and Michael traded punches. Michael had just landed a hard jab. Now, it was Richard's turn. The way he felt right now, he might not stop at one drink, and that scared him. He dialed Angie's number. Voicemail.

"It's Michael. I'm at Winslow's. How soon can you get here?" He ended the call and set the phone on the table.

At the moment, Angie was on his shit list, and he imagined he was on hers, but he'd sensed a deeper bond between them. They had been through some difficult times together. She'd made it clear that, if he ever needed help, she would be there for him. Time to take her up on her offer.

A few minutes later, his drink arrived. He paid the waitress and studied the glass in front of him—so close, he could smell it. The smoky memories returned, and he shuddered. He checked the door. Nothing. *Where are you, Ang?*

Phillip's shiny black Town Car idled at the edge of the parking lot. Emily stopped to look back at the door she'd just walked through. She pictured Michael sitting alone in the booth. *What the hell am I doing?*

Emily stood at the edge of two worlds, suddenly torn between two very different men. She imagined most women in her shoes would hold onto a man like Phillip with both hands. She wasn't most women.

Michael was different. What he may have lacked in social graces, he made up for with sincerity. He was charming in his own way, but she couldn't explain the strange sensation that drew her to him whenever he was around. She'd felt it at the book signing—like she had known him all her life—but that was impossible. Their kiss two weeks ago was so powerful that it frightened her. She'd fought back the feelings, but so far had not been able to eliminate them altogether.

Reluctantly, she continued to walk toward the waiting car. Phillip's driver stepped out as she approached. He reached for the back door handle.

"I can get it myself," she said and let herself in.

Emily folded her arms across her chest. Phillip glanced at her and ended a phone call. Her pulse quickened, and she took a deep breath. The car lunged out of the parking lot and sped off down the boulevard.

"My dear, did you forget our plans tonight?" Phillip's voice was calm and a little condescending.

Emily raised her chin. "We didn't have plans tonight."

"You caught me." He smiled a charming smile. "I warned you to stay away from that Riordan character."

His charming smile wasn't so charming at the moment. "You lied to me."

"Apparently, my dear, you lied to me. I thought we had an agreement."

"That's right, *you* thought. You never asked me what I thought."

He opened his mouth, but no words came out.

"You don't really care what I think, do you?"

Phillip ignored the question. "I've learned to trust my instincts. I have a bad feeling about Michael Riordan. He's dangerous."

"And you're not?" At the moment, Phillip scared her much more than she imagined Michael ever could.

Phillip frowned and rubbed his chin.

"Have you been spying on him, too?"

"I never spied on anyone," he said, the edge gone from his voice. "I care about you, Emily. What's wrong with making sure you're safe?"

"You lied to me," Emily hissed through clenched teeth. "How did you know where I was?"

Again, he ignored her question. "We're together now, and the night is still young. Let's have a few drinks and talk about where you'd like to spend the holidays. How does Aspen sound?"

Emily exhaled sharply and stared out the window. The son-of-a-bitch had elevated dodging questions to an art form. After a few moments, she turned. "Take me home, Phillip."

"I'm only trying to protect—"

"I said, take me home!"

Phillip, his face red with anger, nodded to the driver. A few minutes later, the car pulled up to the curb.

Emily slammed the door and walked up the steps to Lexi's house. Phillip pulled out his cell phone and hit speed-dial.

"Riordan needs to be taught a lesson."

CHAPTER THIRTY-NINE

Michael stared at the amber liquid. He turned the glass around in his hands. It became the only thing in the room—until Tommy slid into the seat across from him.

"You know something, Riordan? You're getting to be a major pain in my ass."

Tommy wore his uniform. Probably just got a call from Phillip. Michael glanced around the room.

"I thought I made myself clear the last time we spoke."

Michael fired back. "Why don't you mind your own goddamn business for a change?"

"You're making this my business," he snarled.

"Emily is my wife, and I have every right to talk to her."

Tommy's eyes narrowed. "I don't know what you're talking about, but it isn't helping your case."

That was an understatement. It appeared nothing could help his case at this point.

"I think you and I should go for a little walk." He showed his Pit Bull teeth.

"I'm busy. Maybe another time." Michael barely heard the words escape his mouth above the hammering in his chest. "I wasn't asking." Tommy's teeth seemed to grow by the minute.

"Michael," Angie called from ten feet away. She stopped at the end of his table.

"Hi, Angie." He attempted to smile, but only managed a flicker. "This is Emily's brother, Tommy." He sent an S.O.S. signal with his eyes.

She glanced at Tommy, they nodded, and she turned back to Michael. "The others will be here in a couple minutes."

"That's great." Michael followed her lead. "Tommy was just leaving." He looked across the table and raised his eyebrows impatiently.

Tommy hesitated, slid out of the seat without a word, and glared down at Angela for a moment before he walked away. Michael watched him leave and waited for the now-familiar gesture. Tommy stopped to flash it just before he walked out the door. Michael tried to steel himself, but a chill ran down his spine. He shook it off and turned to Angie, who had taken Tommy's spot across from him.

"Thanks. You may have just saved my life."

She pointed to the glass in front of him. "How many have you had?"

He nodded his head toward the glass on the table.

"That's your first? Did you drink any?"

"My first Scotch," he said. "I haven't touched it."

She motioned for the waitress to come over and asked her to remove the glass. The waitress looked at Michael.

"Well?" Angie said to Michael with a firm voice.

He nodded to the waitress. She removed the glass and walked away.

"Thank you," Angie said.

"I wasn't sure you'd come."

"I almost didn't," she admitted. "But I couldn't let you fall down that hole again, no matter who you are."

Michael remained silent, but his eyes thanked her.

She put her elbows on the table and leaned in. "So, what happened? Why are you here?"

"I came here with Emily." He stared at the empty table where his drink had been.

She waited for him to continue. "And?"

"It didn't go so well."

"What did you say?"

"I tried to tell her the truth, but I didn't get very far."

"Why not?"

"Prince Phillip came by and collected her. He says 'jump' and she asks 'how high?' I don't get it. It's not like her."

Angie slumped down in her seat and stared at the edge of the table.

"What's the matter, Ang?"

She hesitated. "About the other night…"

"It's okay."

"No, it's not," she insisted. "I'm sorry. It's not the kind of thing you hear every day. Whether I believe you or not, when I look at you, I see my brother." She swiped at a tear that slid down her cheek. "I still don't understand it."

"Angie, I—"

"If you're right, where does that leave me?" She held his gaze.

"A part of him never left." He tapped his chest. "Part of him is sitting right here. You still get to see him whenever you want." He forced a smile with the hope she might reciprocate. She did not.

"I know it's not the same," he continued, "but believe it or not, your friendship means a lot to me. I care about you. Perhaps we can still help each other."

Angie looked away for a moment and then back at Michael. "So, what do we do now?"

"I'm not sure." He sighed. "But I don't want to stay here."

She stood. "Good answer. I don't like this place, either. Let's get the hell out of here."

A sobering thought crossed Michael's mind when he reached his feet. He hesitated momentarily. Was Tommy waiting outside to ambush them in the parking lot?

Angie turned to leave.

He grabbed her arm. "What if Tommy's waiting for us outside?"

Angie reached into her purse. She flashed a Taser and a devious grin.

Tommy leaned back against the door of his police cruiser, arms crossed, and watched the door to Winslow's. This meeting wasn't over. Not by a long shot. His phone rang and he brought it up to his ear.

"No, not yet... I can handle it." Tommy's eyes narrowed and his granite jaw hardened a little more. "I said I'll handle it."

<h1 style="text-align:center">CHAPTER FORTY</h1>

Emily unlocked the front door and let herself in quietly, hoping Lexi had gone to bed early. Roles were reversed—the anxious child waiting for the parent to return home safely. A light burned in the living room. Emily stood in the doorway and watched Lexi turn off the television.

"Goodnight, honey."

Lexi stood. "Mom, wait." She walked toward the doorway. "Are you all right?"

"I'm fine."

Lexi stood in the hall studying her mother. "You look upset."

"It's nothing."

"He didn't hurt you, did he?"

"What?" The question caught her off guard. "Who didn't hurt me?"

"Michael."

Emily frowned. "Why would you think that?"

"Well... you left with him... and... and now you look like something bad happened."

"No, dear. I'm upset with Phillip."

"When did you see Phillip?"

Emily didn't want to admit what she had done to Michael, but the confusion in her daughter's eyes trumped her guilt. "Michael and I went to Winslow's. We were talking when Phillip called from the parking lot, and I left with him." She sighed. "Phillip seems hell-bent on keeping us apart. For all his money and power and good looks, I think he's jealous."

Lexi said nothing.

"I just want to go to bed." She kissed Lexi on the cheek and headed upstairs to the guest room.

Emily closed the bedroom door and thought about what Phillip said. She leaned back against the door, the room dark except for the glow of the digital clock on the bedside table. She'd only had two glasses of wine. She could have used a couple more. She flopped down on the bed and stared at the ceiling. Her Prince Charming was turning back into a frog.

Emily had, for all intents and purposes, ended it with Michael, but apparently like Phillip, he didn't want to take no for an answer. Something was a little off with him, as well. She hated the way she left him at the bar. She had to admit that he'd piqued her curiosity. What was he trying to tell her?

She picked up her phone and dialed Michael's number, but canceled the call before it connected. Maybe she didn't want to know. Emily tossed and turned for the next half-hour. She dialed Michael again, but changed her mind once more. *Look at me! I don't know what the hell I'm doing anymore.* She couldn't trust any of the men in her life, and that was unacceptable.

Morning came too quickly. Emily awoke a few minutes before eight to a knock on the bedroom door. She rubbed the sleep from her eyes.

"Come in," she called.

The door flew open. Kayla ran toward her and jumped up on the bed. "Mornin', Gramma," she chirped. Her infectious smile caused Emily to respond in-kind.

"Good morning, sweetheart."

Kayla scanned the room. "Where's Grampa?"

She hadn't asked about Richard for some time. Emily sat cross-legged on the bed and motioned for her granddaughter to sit in her lap. Kayla responded immediately.

"Remember, honey?" Emily whispered. "Grampa's in heaven." The jury was still out as far as she was concerned, but it's what she'd told Kayla.

"He's back. I saw him." It wasn't a question.

"You saw Grampa? Where?"

"Here. He was with you."

Why was she suddenly talking like this? "No, Kayla, that was Gramma's friend, Michael. Remember?" *You probably won't see him again, either.*

Kayla shook her head from side to side. "No, Gramma. It was Grampa. He called me Lady Bug," she explained with a serious look. "Grampa is the only one who calls me that."

Emily's head spun. There's no way Michael could have known that. She propped up the pillows behind her and leaned back.

"Gramma, are you okay?" Kayla asked, her innocent eyes searching.

"Yes, honey, I'm fine." She leaned forward and cradled her in her arms.

"Is Grampa coming back?"

She squeezed little Lady Bug. "I don't know, honey. I don't know."

Emily made it to work with three minutes to spare. The weekly staff meeting was uneventful, at least the parts Emily remembered. She walked into her boss's office when it was over. She sat and watched him across the messy desk, and waited for him to finish a phone call.

"What can I do for you, Emily?" he asked after he hung up.

"I can't stay here today, Scott," she said. "I don't feel well."

"I thought you looked a little tired in the meeting. Is everything all right?"

"I don't know."

"You realize we're swamped right now. I just received a half-dozen new manuscripts from upstairs." He dropped his hand on a tall stack of papers on the corner of his desk.

"C'mon, Scott, I really feel like crap. I need to go home and sleep."

"You do that. Go home and sleep it off, and you can get started on one of these in the morning."

"I might not be in tomorrow, either."

Scott's expression fell. "What's wrong, Emily?"

"It's... complicated."

"Do you want to talk about it?"

"Thanks, Scott, but I can't. Not now."

"Okay. But, can you do me a favor?"

Emily shrugged.

"Please, just take one of these home with you," he said with a tentative smile. "Who knows? You might want to read something while you're recovering."

"Scott..."

"Please, Emily?"

She sighed. "Okay, what have you got?"

He tapped the pile. "Pick one."

She stood and walked to the corner of his desk, in no mood to make decisions. Hopefully, one of the titles would jump out at her. She picked up the first one. Nope. The second one was mildly interesting. Keep going. Something grabbed her attention when she picked up the third one, but it wasn't the title. The author's name was Michael Riordan.

CHAPTER FORTY-ONE

Michael stopped pacing. He pulled a chair up to Rhonda's desk and sat on the edge of the seat. "She had no right to do that."

Rhonda folded her arms on her desk and leaned in defiantly. "You're lucky she did. They were about to pull the plug."

"You should have asked me before you sent it out. It wasn't finished."

"So, finish it." She waited for a response. When none came, she said, "I had to give them something."

Back on his feet, Michael walked to the window and stared at the street below. "Your friend at the DA's office…" he said without turning around. "It wouldn't be Phillip Morgan, would it?"

"Perhaps I *will* have another look at your car."

Michael turned, but Rhonda avoided his gaze. "If you wait a few minutes, you can watch it driving over to Morgan's office."

A wave of panic washed over her face. "Michael…"

He turned to leave.

"Don't do anything stupid."

Michael didn't look back.

Michael stepped inside the first-floor elevator in the county office building. He stabbed the button for the fifth floor and tapped his foot while he waited for the door to close. He'd built up a head of steam on the ride over. He stabbed the button a couple more times.

By the time the door slid open again, he was halfway down the hall. He entered the offices of Phillip Morgan, Esquire, like a hurricane about to make landfall.

Michael marched past the shapely, blonde receptionist. She pushed her chair back from her desk and stood. He held up his hand to stop her.

"You can't just walk in there," she called after him.

"Watch me." Michael pushed through the large wooden door into Phillip's office. He didn't stop until he reached the middle of the room. The receptionist followed him in and gave Phillip an apologetic shrug.

Phillip, seated in a high-back leather chair behind a large mahogany desk, seemed unaffected by the commotion. "I'm going to have to call you back," he said in a calm voice. He stood, and after a brief pause, instructed the receptionist to close the door on her way out. Phillip offered Michael a seat. Michael refused.

"I know about the accident," Michael announced. He'd been so fired up since he left Rhonda's office, that he hadn't thought about what he would say or how he would say it. "I know what you did."

Phillip smiled an oily smile. "You must have me confused with someone else."

"You know exactly what I'm talking about. And I'm going to bury you with it."

"And you are…?"

"Don't try to pretend you don't know me."

Phillip studied him. "Yes, now I remember. The smartass writer." He pushed some papers around on his desk and added, "Well, whatever it is you think you know—"

"Does the name Richard Dunham ring a bell?"

Phillip struggled to conceal his discomfort.

"How about Rhonda Williams?" Michael let the name hang in the air for a moment. "I understand you two got pretty cozy around the time of the accident."

Phillip stopped what he was doing and folded his hands on his desk. "Perhaps we can arrange some sort of quid pro quo."

Michael didn't go there to make a deal. "The answer is quid pro NO. You're going to stop seeing Emily and tell Tommy to stand down."

This seemed to amuse Phillip, and the smile made another appearance. "And if I don't?"

"You can kiss your chances of becoming DA goodbye."

Phillip didn't move from his pretentious chair behind his pretentious desk. "Have you thought this through, Michael?"

If he had a mustache, he'd be twirling the ends with his oily fingers.

"You have at least as much to lose as I do."

Michael's back stiffened. "I only want what's best for Emily."

Phillip clapped slowly. "That was a stirring performance."

Two security guards rushed in, ready to draw their side-arms if Michael made another move.

Phillip stood and raised a hand. "Everything's under control."

He turned to Michael and said, "We have a deal, Mr. Riordan."

Michael frowned, at a loss for words.

With a grand gesture toward the guards, Phillip said, "These gentlemen will show you out."

Phillip stood at the office window with arms folded across his chest. He watched Michael exit the building below. *Who does he think he is? No one barges into my office and threatens me like that.* He pulled a cell phone from his pocket, tapped the screen and waited.

"I thought I told you to teach him a lesson." He rubbed the back of his neck while he watched Michael slip into the front seat of his car. "That's no excuse."

Phillip turned and walked toward his desk. "He knows too much, and I won't let that little pissant destroy everything I've worked for."

He stopped abruptly. "It's too late for that. Michael Riordan needs to disappear. Permanently."

Phillip ended the call and, with the back of his hand, sent a stack of papers flying from his desk to the floor.

CHAPTER **FORTY-TWO**

Michael stood at the Overlook railing, lost in thought. Phillip had agreed too easily to his demands. Michael had a feeling he'd just poked a huge hornet's nest. Suspicion turned into anxiety while he watched the clouds roll in and cover the park like a low gray ceiling. He turned and hurried down the path.

After two brisk laps around the pond to blow off some steam, he stopped near the clubhouse for a drink of water. Someone called his name when he bent over the fountain. He lifted his head but dismissed the idea that he'd been the intended mark. He heard it again a few moments later.

A familiar figure seated alone at one of the stone chess tables, stared at him from beneath a Red Sox cap. Michael squinted for a better look.

"What are you doing here?" Michael approached the table.

"Did we ever play chess?" he asked with raised eyebrows. "I can't remember."

"I need you to undo whatever it is you did."

Carl studied the blue and silver pieces on the board before he moved one. "As I recall, you left quite a mess."

"I need to clean it up."

"Says the romantic warrior."

"What did you just call me?"

Carl continued to play without looking up. He captured one of the blue pieces—a knight—and held it up to Michael, who took the piece from his hand.

"That move is called a gambit," he explained. "The objective is to sacrifice the knight—the piece you are holding—for a greater advantage." He paused. "You see, in chess, as in life, having the most pieces, or material as they're called, doesn't always provide the greatest advantage."

Michael studied the piece in his hand, then his father.

"Sometimes, Son, it's better to sacrifice some of your material for a higher purpose."

"I'm not here for a chess lesson," Michael snipped. "If you can't help me fix this, then I'll just have to find another way."

"Easy, Spartacus." He looked up from the board. "What makes you think you can fix this now?"

"Now is all I've got."

Carl smiled and gathered the pieces into a pouch. Michael held out the knight.

"You keep it." He stood and placed a hand on Michael's shoulder. "It's never too late to be what you might have been."

Emily returned home from work early. She'd had a rough night and an even rougher morning. Sleep eluded her, and she stared at Michael's manuscript on the nightstand. Three hours later, she finished the last page and frowned. She flipped it over, then back, confused. She set the manuscript down and swung her legs over the side of the bed.

Lexi had just poured a cup of tea when Emily walked into the kitchen.

"You look like you could use a cup," she said to her mother, who pulled a chair from the kitchen table and sat.

Emily nodded.

"Are you sure you're okay?"

"I'm fine, dear."

Lexi set a cup on the table. "I don't believe you."

Emily sipped her tea silently.

"Uncle Tommy stopped by last night."

Emily squinted at Lexi over her cup. "Here? What did he want?"

"He showed me a picture of Michael." She held her mother's gaze. "He wanted to know if I'd ever seen him."

"What did you say?"

"I told him the truth." Lexi hesitated. "How did he know about you and Michael?"

"I might have mentioned it."

"He told me not to worry, but I sensed something was wrong."

Emily did an admirable job of keeping her composure. "I'm sure it was just Uncle Tommy being Uncle Tommy."

"That's what worries me. You know how he can get."

Emily brought the cup to her lips, then set it down.

"Are you going to see him again?"

"I don't know." Emily released the hair she had wrapped around her finger. "Probably not."

Emily returned to her room and climbed back into bed. The manuscript seemed to stare at her from the nightstand and she pulled the covers over her head. Five minutes later, she paced around the room. She picked up her cell phone, stared at it, but didn't dial any numbers. Finally, she changed her clothes, slipped the manuscript into a large purse, and hurried out the door.

CHAPTER **FORTY-THREE**

The rain that had begun to fall on the way home came down harder now. Michael pulled over to the side of the road when he noticed a police cruiser parked in his driveway. The windshield wipers slapped at the gathering rain, and he squinted for a better look. Tommy exited the cruiser and ran for the cover of the front porch. He jiggled the front door handle a couple of times before looking in the window. Michael watched him disappear around the back of the house.

Tommy reappeared a couple minutes later, slipped into his car, and backed out of the driveway. Michael killed the wipers and ducked out of sight as the cruiser sped off past his parked car. When he was sure that Tommy had left the neighborhood, he pulled into his driveway and ran for the front door.

Inside the house, the air felt heavy with impending doom. Michael shook off the rain and checked the front window. He watched the raindrops bounce off the pavement and remembered what Arthur had said that night at the shelter—*Perhaps Emily wanted more.* He remembered the conversation like it was yesterday. They'd been discussing Richard and Emily's relationship, and he'd just told Arthur he was content with the way things were. It was a fair statement, if by content he meant stuck in a rut and too tired or lazy to work his way out. Looking back at it now, it certainly didn't sound like a recipe for a healthy relationship.

Perhaps if he hadn't grown so complacent, so willing to believe Emily would always be there, he wouldn't be in this mess. Was he really that arrogant, as Arthur had put it? He had a different perspective now.

He stepped away from the window, aware that he'd been looking over his shoulder for the past week. Now, he didn't even feel safe in his own home. He retrieved a baseball bat that he'd put in the hall closet and set it near the front door. What had he gotten himself into?

Michael poured himself a drink and set it on the kitchen counter, then walked into his office to check the lock on the French doors. He opened the desk drawer and retrieved the photo of Richard and Emily that Arthur had given him. Winning Emily back would be a challenge, but he never imagined he'd have to physically fight for her. This Tommy thing had gotten out of hand.

The doorbell rang, and he shoved the photo into his pocket.

"Shit!" Tommy must have circled back and seen his car in the driveway. He ran to the front door and grabbed the baseball bat. He took a deep breath, held the bat high in the air, and opened the door.

Angie flinched. "Again with the Rambo act? Michael, what the hell is going on?"

"Now's not a good time, Ang." He set the bat down.

She took a step inside. "Something's going on, and I want to know what it is."

Michael wrapped his arms around his sister. "Thank you."

"For what?"

"For being you."

"Who else would I be?" Angie stared at Michael through squinted eyes. "Are you sure you're OK?"

"I thought you might be…" He glanced back toward the kitchen where he'd left the open bottle of Scotch. "I'll talk to you tomorrow."

Angie tried to look past him. "Is someone else in there?"

"Thanks for stopping by. Talk tomorrow." Michael pushed her through the door and closed it behind her.

He walked into the kitchen and threw back the drink he'd poured earlier. Before he picked up the bottle again, someone pounded on the front door. "I mean it, Ang. Not now."

Michael shook his head and walked toward the door as the pounding continued. He yanked open the door. "I'm not kidding. You need to—"

"I need to what?" Tommy growled.

Michael glanced at the bat that stood just out of his reach. He mustered a steely glare. "What do you want?"

"To make sure you don't cause any more trouble." He thrust an index finger toward Michael's chest. Michael slapped his hand away before it reached its target.

Tommy looked surprised by the quick response, but it didn't last long. He pushed his way inside. Michael rocked back on his heels and took a couple of steps backward to keep his balance. He glanced again at the bat, farther away now.

"What do you want?" Michael demanded when he regained his balance.

Tommy looked past Michael into the living room. "Where's all the boxes?"

"Boxes?"

"I thought you'd be in here packing up your shit." His eyes held equal parts of disappointment and pure evil.

The thought of being run out of town sent Michael's stomach into a spin.

"I gotta tell you, Riordan." Tommy shook his head slowly. "I'm a little disappointed."

"Well, get used to it," Michael said. "I'm not going anywhere."

Tommy's eyes grew wild for a second before a grin slowly spread across his lips. "Hmmm…" He rubbed his chin. "Maybe that's not such a bad thing, after all. It just means I finally get to mess you up."

Michael needed to act quickly, or that's most likely what would happen. While he considered his options, a car pulled into the driveway, and Tommy turned his head to take a look. Michael reached in his pocket for his keys, made a fist, and slid his car key between his fingers. With Tommy distracted, Michael lunged for his throat.

Michael had hesitated a fraction of a second, and it cost him. Tommy turned around quickly and deflected the attack. He grabbed Michael by the neck with his right hand and pushed him up against the wall.

"I thought you were smarter than that, Riordan," he said through clenched teeth.

Michael attempted to speak, but no words made it past Tommy's hand.

"You thought that little stunt in the parking lot with the Taser was funny, didn't you?" Tommy smiled an evil smile. "Payback's a bitch."

"Tommy!" a voice called from the open doorway.

Tommy's head spun around. "Emily! What the hell are you doing here?" He held his grip on Michael's neck.

Still pinned against the wall, unable to speak, Michael's eyes moved to find Emily's.

"Let him go."

Tommy loosened his grip on Michael's neck. "No. He jumped me."

"What are you going to do, beat him up?"

Tommy snickered. "For starters."

Emily placed her hands on her hips. "You need to leave."

She looked at Michael, her expression unreadable. He swallowed hard but said nothing.

Emily convinced Tommy to let Michael go. He pulled her inside and slammed the door behind her. He pushed Michael into the living room. Emily followed, voicing her protest. She glared at Tommy, who made it clear he wasn't leaving.

She turned to Michael. "You'd better start talking, or I'm going to let the two of you work this out alone."

CHAPTER **FORTY-FOUR**

"I wanted to tell you everything," Michael explained, "but I was afraid it would scare you off."

"Do you really think I want to be with a man who's afraid to tell me the truth? I did that once. It didn't turn out well."

Emily reached into her purse and pulled out Michael's manuscript. "While we're on the subject of full disclosure, what do you have to say about this?"

"What's that?" Tommy asked.

Michael knew. But how did it end up in Emily's purse?

"Well, Michael?"

Instead of answering, he said, "Where did you get that?"

"I'll ask the questions."

"I tried to tell you at Winslow's."

"There's a lot of personal information in here." She waved the manuscript at him. "How did you know Richard?"

Michael hesitated. "I'm not sure how to answer that."

"Let's start with the truth."

Angie's voice echoed in his mind. *Don't be such a pussy.*

"You want the truth?" Michael's back stiffened. "It's more of a memoir than a work of fiction." Time to come clean—do or die. "I didn't just know Richard. I am Richard. I came back for you, Emily."

Emily looked at Tommy for help, then back to Michael. "What? That's impossible."

"You're my reason to live."

Tommy's eyes darted back and forth between Emily and Michael. "What's he talking about?"

Emily held up a hand. "Shut up, Tommy!"

Tommy showed some teeth. "Let me see that."

Emily tossed the manuscript to Tommy, and he moved to catch it. Michael seized the opportunity. He picked up a brass lamp from the end table and swung it at Tommy's head. Tommy dodged the attack and grabbed Michael. The two struggled.

"Tommy, stop!"

Michael and Tommy bounced off the wall.

Emily yelled, "Richard!"

Michael froze. His eyes met Emily's. Time stood still for them, but not for Tommy. He landed a punch that sent Michael to the floor.

Emily gasped. She knelt at Michael's side and held up her hand as Tommy approached.

He stopped and looked down at them. "You should have left when I told you."

Emily grabbed one of Michael's arms. "Shut up and help me."

Tommy helped her pull Michael to a sitting position against the sofa. Michael yanked his arm away from Tommy and winced in pain.

"Who are you?" Emily asked Michael.

He rubbed his sore chin. "I'm your romantic warrior."

Emily's mouth fell open and her eyes widened. "What... what did you say?"

Michael pulled the photo from his pocket. Emily snatched it from his hand.

"I remember the first time I saw you..." he whispered.

She studied the photo.

"Walking through the campus quad. You turned and smiled at me, and... I knew my life would never be the same."

Emily continued to stare at the photo.

Michael's body shuddered. He gasped and clutched his chest.

"What's the matter?"

"I don't know." He reached for a breath, and fear washed over his eyes. The edges of his vision faded into a different scene, like another reality existed behind what his eyes showed him. He heard muffled voices, but he saw no one else in the room.

Emily watched with fear in her eyes.

"I came back to..." Michael focused on Emily, and his vision stabilized momentarily. "...to be the man you wanted me to be."

Tommy rolled his eyes. "For God's sake, Emily."

Emily looked at Tommy, then back to Michael.

"Please, Em. Say something," he whispered.

Emily reached out a trembling hand and pressed her palm to Michael's cheek. "I don't understand. How...?"

An electric shock took Michael's breath away, and he shuddered again. He winced and grabbed his chest. A ragged breath was all he could manage as he stared vacantly into Emily's eyes.

"My romantic warrior." Emily wiped a tear. "Don't leave me again, Richard."

The muffled voices were back, louder this time. He felt the room move just before blackness engulfed his vision and swallowed him whole.

An IV bag swung from a post as the ambulance cornered hard. An EMT leaned over Richard's bare chest, defibrillator paddles held high.

The second EMT studied a portable heart monitor. "No change."

"Push Epi. Charge to 300." He lowered the paddles again. "Clear!"

Richard's body jumped. Everyone waited in silence. The monitors came alive with a steady beat.

"Sinus rhythm."

They pulled into the ambulance bay three minutes later. A doctor and nurse approached as the ambulance backed in. The doors swung open, and the EMTs jumped out. Stretcher legs dropped and locked when they pulled Richard from the ambulance.

"MVA. Richard Dunham. Approximately forty-five-year-old male. Non-responsive at the scene. Stabilized en route, but he was down for almost two minutes. BP 90 over 40."

Large glass doors slid open with a *whoosh*. Richard watched the ceiling while the team rushed him to a trauma room. An ER doctor slipped his hand into a pair of latex gloves to perform his examination.

"You're a lucky man, Mr. Dunham."

Richard stared at the doctor. "What?"

"I said, you're a lucky man. You flipped your car, and I understand they had to cut you out." He took another look into Richard's eyes with a small pen light.

Richard pushed his hand away. "You called me Mr. Dunham."

The doctor took a half step backward as he studied his patient. "That's your name, isn't it?"

Richard couldn't be sure. "Uh… yes, yes of course."

The exam lasted another ten minutes before the doctor peeled off his gloves in a corner of the room. A nurse walked in.

"He's stable. No broken bones," he said to the nurse. "I ordered a CT scan."

He wrote something in the chart. "I'm going to keep him overnight for observation." He handed her the chart. "I'll check on him in the morning."

She nodded.

Richard watched the doctor leave the room. "I need a mirror," he said to the nurse.

"What for?"

He didn't have time for Q and A. He needed to see if it was true. "Do you have one or don't you?"

"I'm sorry."

He sat up. "What color are my eyes?" He spoke a little too loudly.

She studied him silently like he was a mental patient. "Please lie back down or I'll have to call security."

Richard saw the fear gathering in her eyes. He held up his hands. "OK. I'm sorry." He laid his head back on the table. "I'll behave. Please. Just look at my eyes and tell me what color they are."

She took a hesitant step forward and leaned in. "Your eyes are brown."

Elevator doors opened and Emily and Samantha stepped off. They glanced at the numbers on the wall, then turned down the hall toward Richard's room. They found Richard asleep, and Carolyn at his bedside. She held his hand. Emily and Samantha stopped in the doorway. They looked at each other briefly before Samantha pulled Emily back.

"That's the woman I saw him with at the restaurant."

Emily's eyes widened. *The little black dress.* "I need to talk to her."

Sam grabbed Emily's arm when she took a step toward the door.

"Do you think that's a good idea?"

"No." She pulled her arm away. "But—"

Samantha pushed Emily past the doorway before she could step into the room. She grabbed Emily's arm again and pulled her down the hall.

Emily resisted and they stopped. "What'd you do that for?"

"You really don't know?"

Emily looked back toward the room, then to Samantha. "I just want to…"

Sam shook her head. "Bad idea, Em."

"But I need to—"

"You need to go home. He's asleep. We can come back in the morning."

Emily chewed her bottom lip for a moment, then nodded.

Sam led her by the arm down the hall away from the room.

Emily resisted. "The elevator is back that way."

"We'll find another way out."

CHAPTER **FORTY-FIVE**

The front doors of the hospital slid open, and a nurse pushed Richard's wheelchair out onto the sidewalk.

"Is this really necessary?"

"Hospital policy."

A taxi pulled up to the curb. Richard stood, thanked the nurse, and slid into the back seat.

On the ride home, he thought about what he would say to Emily. Yesterday seemed like a lifetime ago. He still couldn't believe it had come to this. These things happened to other couples, not to them. He had to find a way to turn it around. This was a new day, and in some ways, a new Richard. The past was, well, the past. What he did next is all that mattered.

The taxi pulled into his driveway, and he stared through the window at the coach lamp that Lexi had broken playing basketball two... no, three summers ago. Was it really that long? He made a mental note to replace it, and exited the vehicle.

Everything appeared as he remembered, but he couldn't shake the feeling that something was different. Perhaps he's the one who had changed. Whatever he felt, he didn't understand it yet. He struggled to sort out reality from... he wasn't sure what to call it. He shoved his hands into his pockets and walked around to the back of the house. Memories flashed by, but could they be trusted?

He climbed the stairs to the deck.

Emily didn't get up from her seat under an umbrella. "What are you doing here?"

"I'm fine, thank you."

"I'm not."

Richard sat in the chair across from her. "Can I at least have my day in court before I'm convicted?"

Emily folded her arms impatiently.

"I'm sorry, Em. I fell asleep at the switch, but I'm awake now. You're looking at Richard 2.0."

"People don't change overnight."

"That's what I used to think. But it feels like I lived a lifetime last night."

Richard's phone vibrated in his pocket, and Emily waited. He stared at Carolyn's name on the screen, then dismissed the call.

"Was that her?"

Richard looked up. "Who?"

"Richard, please... I may be naive, but I'm not stupid. Samantha saw you with her at the restaurant. Then she's at your bedside last night holding your hand?"

"The nurse told me a woman visited during the night." He sighed. "I'd hoped it was you."

"Was she with you in the car?"

He replied with an emphatic, "No."

"It's obvious she has feelings for you."

"That doesn't matter. You're the only woman I've ever loved, Em."

She ignored his previous comment. "You were with her the night of our anniversary."

He shifted his weight in his chair. "It's not what you think. I needed to talk to her about a financial problem."

"Why would you go to her with a problem instead of me?"

Richard moved to the edge of his chair. "Because she was the problem. I screwed up, Em, and I didn't have the courage to tell you." He hesitated. "The money we saved. It was gone. So was the line of credit. I panicked."

"What?"

"Carolyn offered to bail me out, and I took her money. I didn't have the courage to tell you what happened."

"Why would she do that?"

"She wanted something in return."

"And you gave it to her. Didn't you?"

He held up his hands. "No, no. I realized I couldn't do that to you. When I told her I couldn't go through with it, she read me a letter she wrote full of lies intended to tear us apart. The accident happened on my way home to tell you the truth."

Emily exhaled sharply. "Why should I believe you?

"I swear. Nothing happened."

"Where's the money now."

"I'm going to pay it back. Every cent. Then I swear I'll never speak to her again."

Emily's slumped back in her chair. "How could you gamble with our savings?"

"Carolyn said it was a sure thing. I thought all that extra money would make you happy."

"It's not always about money," she said as if everyone should know that.

Richard nodded.

"It's always been about you, and your job, and your stupid car."

Richard avoided her eyes.

"I have dreams, too. Don't get me wrong, I loved being a mom, but Lexi's gone now, and I need to focus on me."

"I won't hold you back. Whatever you want to do, I'll support you one-hundred percent."

"Did you ever hear the expression, *Too little, too late*?"

"I prefer, *It's never too late to be who you might have been.*"

Emily stared at her hands in her lap.

"Can you forgive me?"

"I'm not ready to do that just yet."

"Why not?"

"You've been phoning it in for a while now. I'm just not a priority anymore. And with everything that's happened in the last few days... I need some time."

"How much time?

"You left me alone on our anniversary to think about you doing God-knows-what with another woman... a beautiful woman."

"I told you. Nothing happened."

Richard held her gaze, and for a moment, neither of them said anything.

"Do you know how hard it was to push you away, to make you leave like that?" Her eyes narrowed. "It was a huge step—one I never wanted to take. But now that I have, I'm not willing to undo it too hastily. I need to be sure."

Bogey walked over to Richard, who stroked his head and scratched behind his ear. "What do you think, boy?"

"He doesn't get a vote."

Richard looked up at Emily. "I'm going to find a way to make it up to you, Em. I promise."

"Right now, the only thing you need to find is your way out. Please... just go." Emily stood, turned, and disappeared into the house.

Richard walked to the driveway, Bogey at his side. His hand gently followed the contour of the Blue Knight's fender as he walked around to the front of the car. He let out a sigh of relief. If not for the busted timing chain, he would have been driving this car on that fateful night.

"Let's get this baby back on the road," he said to Bogey, then popped the hood.

Emily, hands on her hips, watched from the kitchen. She shook her head slowly, then turned away.

CHAPTER FORTY-SIX

Emily pushed her food around on her plate, so lost in thought that it took a moment to realize her phone was ringing. She decided dinner was over, walked to the counter, and picked up the phone.

"You've got to tell me what's been going on over there," Samantha said.

"What do you mean?"

"I just got a delivery. Flowers. From Richard."

Emily turned around and leaned back against the counter. "Richard? Why would he do that?"

Samantha hesitated. "We had a little chat at Frank's party. Well, he didn't actually say anything. I read him the riot act, Em. I told him I knew what he was up to and—"

"Did you?"

"Did I what?"

"Know what he was up to?"

"I told you about that night at the restaurant. Isn't it obvious?"

"I'm not so sure."

"The note with the flowers said he was sorry and that he told you everything. So, come on. Spill it."

Emily paused while she decided how much to tell her. "He was hiding something, but I don't think it was an affair."

Samantha waited. "Well?"

"He invested all the money we saved and lost it."

"And you knew nothing about this... investment?"

"Nope. He never said a word."

"He must have crapped his pants."

"Small consolation."

"So how did he know that woman? I told you, she was pretty hot."

"He admitted being there with her that night. She's a client of his. She was in on the investment. Apparently, they were celebrating how well they'd done before the whole thing went south."

"Do you think he slept with her?"

"I'm not sure."

"What are you going to do?"

"I don't know, Sam. This whole thing has made me think about a lot of things."

"What are you thinking about? Divorce?"

The word hung there for a moment. "Is that what you're hoping?" Emily asked.

"No, absolutely not. I wouldn't wish that on anybody." Sam took a deep breath and Emily waited. "Even though you're my little sister, I've always looked up to you, maybe even envied you for what you've done with your life. After my divorce, it became obvious that you had what I wanted. I guess it's why I've been so hard on Richard. Now, I don't know what to think."

"Misery loves company, right?"

"It's not like that, Em. I guess I thought that if it could happen to someone like you, then maybe I wasn't such a loser, after all."

In her entire life, Emily had never heard her sister cry. "Sam?"

"I'm sorry, Em."

"It's okay." She sighed. "I'm not thinking about divorce. At least, not at the moment. I'm thinking more about who I am. I don't even know any more. Richard and I have been together so long, and now that Lexi's gone, I need to figure it out."

Neither said anything for a moment.

"Perhaps that's what Richard has been doing." Samantha offered.

Emily sighed. "You think?"

"I love you, Sis, and I'll support you whichever way this goes."

"Thanks, Sam. I love you, too," Emily whispered. She set the phone down and closed her eyes.

Richard sat, head in hands, across the desk from a young loan officer who looked like he'd rather be playing shortstop than sitting behind a desk and serving up bad news to his former Little League coach. The advance Richard had requested against his Home Equity Line of Credit had been denied. No surprise there. He'd taken a hefty advance to double down on the *sure thing* with Carolyn.

"Coach Dunham? You okay?"

The stiff cushion and sterile decor offered little comfort. Richard raised his head. "It's not your fault."

The young man shrugged. "There's really nothing I can do. Your line of credit is maxed out and you're behind a couple of payments. If you don't make some kind of payment soon—"

"How old are you, Davey?"

"Twenty-five."

"What I wouldn't give to be twenty-five again." Richard shook his head. "I'm gonna turn forty-five this year." He raked his hand back through his salt and pepper hair. "But I'm not afraid of that number. It's the numbers on my bank statement that keep me up at night."

Davey nodded, then smiled a boyish smile. "You're still my hero."

"No. You got me all wrong. I'm a cautionary tale at best."

"You've always been more like a father to me than a coach."

"I like to think I set a good example when I was your coach, and maybe I taught you boys something. But if I ever try to give you financial advice, you better run the other way."

Davey glanced at the papers on his desk, then offered a sympathetic smile. "I guess I won't argue with you there."

"Are you sure there's nothing else you can do?"

"I wish there was. I've stuck my neck out so far on this one that it's halfway out the door." He swallowed hard. "I have a wife and kid now."

"I know something about wives and kids. You do what you gotta do."

"I'm sorry, Coach."

Richard stood and put a hand on the young man's shoulder. "Don't waste any time worrying about me, son. I got myself in a bit of a jam, but I'm going to find my way out of it."

CHAPTER **FORTY-SEVEN**

Richard hadn't heard from Emily in two days. He wanted to give her some space, but he also wanted to keep the lines of communication open. She spent more time with Samantha, and he was pretty sure that didn't help his case. He drove to the house and found her washing dishes at the kitchen sink. He watched for a moment through the screen before he knocked.

"Come in," she called.

He never imagined he'd have to knock on his own door, but he'd agreed to respect Emily's privacy while they figured out how to proceed. He believed it would be a temporary arrangement. They made small talk while she continued with the dishes.

Richard cleared his throat. "I feel like you've been avoiding me."

"I know the feeling."

"Guess I deserve that." He hesitated. "But I don't want to throw it all away because of a... a misunderstanding. Do you?"

Richard waited for a response that didn't come. He walked to where she stood and leaned against the counter. "I'd like to move back in. Not everyone is lucky enough to have what we had... have. I don't want to lose that, Em."

Emily picked up a towel and dried her hands. "I wish you felt that way two years ago." She walked to the kitchen table and sat down.

"So do I," he admitted and sat in the chair next to hers. "The sad part is, I did. I just didn't know it. I lost sight of what really mattered. I made a careless mistake. One I won't make again."

"You told me you would always be there for me... and you weren't. That feels like betrayal."

Richard couldn't un-ring that bell. The damage had been done. It wasn't even about the money anymore. He needed to prove she could trust him again. He needed to make her feel safe. "I'm sorry, Em."

"Why did it take you so long?"

Richard looked away. "What if everything Arthur said was true?" he asked after an awkward silence. "What if I was given a glimpse of what the future might be like if I continue down the same road?"

"Arthur?"

"The old man I told you about from the shelter."

"Do you know how crazy that sounds, Richard?"

"Of course, I do," he said. His eyes widened and he leaned forward in his chair. "But I was there. It was real. I've been missing the point. It's a wonderful life if you appreciate what you have. I haven't been doing that."

"I can't argue with you there." She breathed a heavy sigh. "I've racked my brain to find a subtle, yet compelling, way to get through to you. Then you talk to some homeless person one night and suddenly you 'get it'? How do you think that makes me feel?"

"I don't know... grateful?"

"Did you even hear what I just said?"

"I heard you. Does it matter how I get there, as long as I get there?"

Emily walked to the kitchen window. She looked outside for a moment, then turned. She leaned back against the counter and folded her arms across her chest. Richard left the table and wrapped his arms around her. She lowered her head, arms still folded in front of her.

"I want to be *us* again."

Emily nodded.

He kissed the top of her head before he let her go. "So, what do you think?"

"About what?"

"About me moving back."

"I'm sorry, Richard." She looked away for a moment. "I'm not saying it won't happen... just not now."

"C'mon, Em—"

"No. All this happened for a reason. Maybe it's not just about you. Maybe I need a break, too. I've been feeling a little lost, like I don't know who I am anymore."

"Why can't we figure it out together?"

"It's something I have to do on my own."

The vulnerability in her eyes disarmed him. He waited for an explanation, but she seemed to feel no need to elaborate. He accepted her answer without further debate.

It could have all gone down like dominoes with one more push, but he wasn't going to let that happen. He didn't get the answer he wanted, but what he got was encouraging. Richard took a few steps toward the door before he turned around. "When can I see you again?"

"I know it's hard to believe, but my social calendar is pretty open." Her lips twitched in a weak smile. "Oh, except for Saturday night." Her eyes locked on to his. "I have a date."

He raised his eyebrows as if to say, *You've got to be kidding.* "A date?"

"Do you have a problem with that?"

"Well, I..."

"Relax." Despite the tension, Emily smiled. "I'm going out with Samantha. It's just some political fundraiser."

Richard exhaled. "Since when are you interested in politics?"

"I'm not, but it's for a friend of Tommy's, so Sam and I agreed to go. It's not like I have anything better to do on a Saturday night."

Richard swallowed hard. "A friend of Tommy's?"

"Yeah, some freakishly handsome guy who's running for District Attorney."

"You can't go," he blurted out.

"Excuse me?"

"Uh... what I mean is... I've got something special planned... for us, for Saturday." He lied. He had to convince her to cancel her plans.

She looked at him curiously. "What is it?"

"I can't tell you. It's a surprise."

"Really?" She tilted her head. "Are you asking me out on a date? I'm not sure I remember what that sounds like."

He ignored her sarcasm and smiled. "It's more than a date. But you won't know unless you go."

"Can we do it some other night? I promised Sam—"

"No. It has to be Saturday."

She wrinkled her brow. "If you're trying to make up for our anniversary—"

"I apologize for my careless oversight, but that was the past."

Silence.

"So?"

"I'll think about it," she said.

Still a tough nut to crack.

CHAPTER **FORTY-EIGHT**

Emily set a glass of iced tea on a table in a small outdoor café, hoping she'd made the right decision.

"So, you took me to lunch to let me down easy. Is that it?"

"No... well, maybe," Emily admitted.

"I was really looking forward to Saturday night."

"You were looking forward to not walking in there alone." Emily knew her sister had an ulterior motive for inviting her to the swanky affair after Sam offered to pay her way. "I know you, Sam. After the first drink, you'll drop me like a bad habit and start working the room."

"That hurts, Emily." Samantha lowered her eyes and waited.

Emily remained silent.

Sam raised her head and flashed a devious grin. "I'll have you know, I planned to stick around for two drinks this time."

"Well then, I just might have to reconsider," Emily said, and they both laughed.

Sam finished the last bite of her sandwich and washed it down with some iced tea. Her expression became serious. "Believe it or not, I understand, Em. You have to do what you think is right. It's different than Matt and me. You still have a chance."

"I know," she sighed, "but now it appears I'm the one who has to make the final decision. I hate that kind of pressure."

Samantha's eyes darted back and forth, and she leaned in closer to Emily. "I know. You want to make the right decision." She lowered her voice. "That's why I had Tommy look into Richard's activity over the past few months."

"What?"

Samantha leaned back. "I wasn't going to risk my job for something like that, but Tommy—"

"Sam!" Emily glared. "I thought I told you—"

Samantha held up her hands. "Too late. It's done." They stared at each other in silence. "Do you want to know what he found or don't you?"

Emily knew she should say no, but… "I don't know, Sam."

"Relax," she said. "It's good news."

Emily remained silent, but her eyes told Sam to continue.

Samantha explained that Tommy had found nothing suspicious in Richard's phone records or credit card receipts. "Carolyn's number showed up a few times, but I think we can assume it was about that investment thing. Other than that, I think he's been behaving." She smiled.

"It feels a little sleazy, you know, checking up on him that way, but I guess I'm relieved to hear what you found."

"You're welcome."

Emily forced a smile. She finished her tea and chewed on a piece of ice as she stared past Samantha.

"You want my advice?" Sam asked.

Emily's gaze met hers.

Sam didn't wait for her to answer. "Take it slow. Don't rush into anything. If he's sincere and this is what he truly wants, he'll wait for you."

"I suppose you're right. There's no hurry." Her eyes drifted. "He still needs to prove himself before I let him back."

The devious grin returned to Samantha's face. "You might want to make him sweat a little. You know, show him—"

"That's enough, Sam." Emily rolled her eyes. "I get the point." She reached for her purse.

"So, what time do you want me to pick you up Saturday night?" Sam asked.

Emily looked at her sideways.

Sam held up her hands. "You can't blame a girl for trying."

Richard leaned against the rail of the Overlook and watched the activity below—business as usual. Everyone acted so normal. He thought about how his life had become anything but normal.

A young couple stood on the other side of the platform, and Richard couldn't help but steal a glance every now and then. They spoke in hushed tones and gazed into each other's eyes. It reminded him of the times he and Emily had stood in the very same spot.

He didn't love her any less now; in fact, he loved her more. A deeper love, one that came from a place of understanding that they meant more to each other than a simple human relationship. They were soul mates. That's what Arthur said. They had a cosmic connection that wasn't limited to this lifetime. Sure, it sounded a little out there, but lately, out there had become much closer.

Now he stood on the Overlook alone, formulating a plan to win back Emily's heart. Back? How could he have lost it? It didn't matter now. He knew what he had to do. He just wasn't quite sure how to pull it off. Emily was the most important thing in his life, his reason to live, and he had to make sure she knew that. Given their current situation, it seemed like a tall order. However, he would not be discouraged. Where there's a will, there's a way... and there is definitely a will.

He scanned the park below, his eyes drawn to a man in a Red Sox cap who sat alone at one of the chess tables. Richard squinted for a better look, then took off down the path.

Richard's shoulders sagged when he reached the tables and found them empty. They'd only been out of his sight for a minute or two on his way down from the Overlook—not enough time for someone to pack up and leave. He searched for any signs of activity. Nothing. Here one minute, gone the next. The man was a ghost.

He shoved his hands in his pockets and turned to leave. He stopped when he felt the chess piece. Richard didn't know much about the game of chess, but he remembered what his father had said when he'd first showed the piece to Michael. He'd made a move where he intentionally sacrificed that piece. A gambit, he called it—part of a larger strategy.

"That's it!" he said aloud. How could I have missed it? He stared at the blue knight in what Emily would call an *aha moment*. Without hesitation, he pulled his cell phone from his pocket, scrolled through his list of contacts, and tapped one of them. Moments later, Richard smiled and ended the call.

"Thanks, Dad," he whispered, then slipped the phone into his pocket and left the park in a hurry.

CHAPTER **FORTY-NINE**

A black limousine pulled up in front of Emily's house at exactly seven o'clock on Saturday night. The driver exited the vehicle and opened the rear door. Richard stepped into the street and buttoned his jacket.

His breath caught in his throat when Emily opened her front door. She wore an off-the-shoulder, champagne-colored dress that shimmered in the evening sun. She hadn't worn it since Lexi's wedding, and he remembered how he'd been unable to take his eyes off her at the reception. They made love that night when they returned home.

"I'm sorry," he said.

Her expression went blank. "Sorry? For what?"

"I'd forgotten how absolutely beautiful you are."

Emily smiled briefly before lowering her gaze. "Thank you, Richard."

He offered his arm. "Shall we?"

Champagne and roses awaited them in the limo. Richard instructed the driver to take the scenic route.

The limo eventually pulled to a stop in front of *Autour du Monde*, and Emily glanced out the window then back to Richard. "This is a surprise."

He flashed a confident smile. "Expect the unexpected."

She held his gaze. The driver walked around the car and opened their door. Richard placed his hand on the small of her back, and they walked toward the restaurant.

"Bonsoir." The doorman smiled as he tilted his head and held open the door.

Emily returned the smile. Richard nodded and followed her in.

Small wooden tables sat on a checkered tile floor. The plaster walls and wainscoting showed their age gracefully in the low light. Richard half-expected to catch a glimpse of the Eiffel Tower through the front window. They walked past the bar to the main dining room where the maître d' greeted them.

The room was elegantly appointed without sacrificing any of the old-world charm. Tables for two with fresh flowers on white linen sat beneath reproductions of famous French paintings. Muted colors and soft lighting added to the intimate atmosphere. The maître d' held Emily's chair, and she sat, her eyes wide and sparkling.

She unfolded her napkin and placed it on her lap while she glanced around the busy room. "I heard it takes months to get a reservation here. How did you—?"

"I had a little help," he admitted.

Emily was right. You couldn't just call *Autour du Monde* and get a reservation for Saturday night, but Richard knew someone who could. Actually, he knew someone who knew someone.

At first, Tommy McKenna had not been happy to hear from Richard. Surprised, but not happy. Richard explained his side of the story while Tommy listened. After Richard made his case for a reconciliation, Tommy reluctantly agreed to help him out. He told Richard that he had a good friend with enough juice to get him a reservation for Saturday night.

"I've got to say, Richard." Emily looked around the room. "This is not hurting your case."

"Did I tell you I called my sister?"

She tilted her head and frowned. "Now you're really freakin' me out. You haven't spoken to Julie in ten years. What's going on?"

A broad smile crossed his face. "Freaked her out, too."

Emily leaned forward, her expression playful. "Who are you, and what have you done with my husband?"

A fair question, he thought. "Richard 2.0," he reminded her, feeling hopeful. "The upgrade was long overdue."

Richard had pulled out all the stops. The restaurant was just the beginning. They took their time with dinner—the best meal either one of them had eaten in a long time; maybe ever. Likewise, conversation was the most comfortable it had been for some time. They ordered Cherries Jubilee for dessert and another drink after the table had been cleared. His plan seemed to be working.

From the corner of his eye, Richard noticed a familiar face, and his dessert nearly made a second appearance. Phillip Morgan wore a suit that probably cost more than Richard's car. He crossed the room, stopped at their table, and looked down at Emily.

"You must be Emily," he said.

She glanced at Richard then back. "Yes. I am. Have we met?"

"My name is Phillip Morgan."

Richard shifted uncomfortably in his seat.

Phillip turned. "I'm sorry." He held out his hand. "Phillip Morgan, Assistant District Attorney."

Richard hesitated. He assumed that Phillip was the friend Tommy used to secure their reservation, but this scene brought back unpleasant memories. He took his hand and cleared his throat. "Richard Dunham."

"I'm sorry to intrude, but I just wanted to make sure Pascal took good care of you."

Richard nodded. "Everything's perfect."

"Enjoy the rest of your evening."

"We will," Richard said, and watched him walk away.

When he turned to Emily, she stared at him with wide eyes. "What was that about?"

A faint smile played on his lips. "Like I said, expect the unexpected."

When they left the restaurant, Richard instructed the driver to kill some time before their next stop. He held the champagne bottle up to the light. Enough for a couple of glasses remained. They settled into the soft leather seats, and he offered a toast to a new beginning. Emily smiled, but said nothing. Their glasses met and he quickly emptied his.

Richard reached into his breast pocket. "I have a present for you," he said with a nervous smile and held an envelope between them.

Emily set down her glass. Her eyes narrowed. "What for?"

"No reason. Just something I thought you might like."

"First dinner... and now a gift." She tilted her head. "If I didn't know better, I'd say that you were trying to—"

"Go ahead, open it."

Emily took the envelope, slid the contents out, and examined it. She drew in a quick breath and looked at Richard, eyes wide.

CHAPTER **FIFTY**

"We leave next week," Richard said. "You can cross it off your bucket list."

"I don't know what to say."

"How about: This is awesome, Richard… I'll start packing as soon as I get home?"

"I wish I could say that... but I can't." Emily's expression fell. "I can't just jet off to Ireland…"

"Why not?"

"I'm sure I couldn't get time off from work on such short notice."

"I thought you might say that." He smiled. "I talked to Scott, and he agreed to give you the time off."

She held the tickets to her chest, closed her eyes and took a deep breath. Her bottom lip trembled, and she lowered her head. He waited patiently for a response, then placed a hand on her shoulder. She didn't resist.

Richard attempted to make eye contact. "Em?"

She opened her eyes without looking up. "Do you really think this is a good time to do something like this?"

The smile slid off his face. His head told him: *Maybe she's right. Maybe I'm rushing things.* That's when his heart stepped in. "Absolutely. It's the perfect time. Think of it as a turning point. A new beginning, new memories."

Emily twirled a lock of hair around her finger.

"I know there are places you want to see and people you want to meet," he said. "You can do it all. I won't hold you back from any of it. It's what you said you've always wanted. Let me give that to you."

He didn't like what he saw in her eyes.

"Of course, it sounds wonderful." She looked down at the tickets and then back at him. "But I'm just not sure we're ready for this."

"Please, Em, what's it going to take?"

"I know we can't afford to do this. How did you even pay for these tickets?"

He winked. "A magician never reveals his secrets."

"But Richard—"

"No buts. Just say yes."

She hesitated. "I'm scared."

"What are you afraid of, Em?"

"What am I afraid of?" She had that look in her eyes again. "I'm afraid I'm being naive if I blindly trust this sudden change of heart."

He paused, looking her in the eyes. "I know it's a lot to ask, but—"

"Why did it take something so drastic to make you understand?" Her head moved slowly from side to side. "I have to protect myself, Richard. I can't let this happen again."

"Is that what love is about now... protecting yourself?"

She placed the envelope in his hand.

"Will you at least think about it, Em?"

"Yes, Richard. I'll think about it."

He opened the envelope, examined the two tickets, and slipped one of them into the pocket of her purse. "I'll be on that plane, Emily. I guess the rest is up to you." He leaned over and kissed her forehead as the car came to a stop in front of The Paradise Club.

Emily looked out the window, then down to her lap. "Richard, I don't feel much like dancing tonight."

"C'mon, Em. The night is still young."

"Let's not spoil a lovely evening," she said, her voice firm.

His stomach told him that it might be a little late for that.

The driver remained in the car when they reached the house. Richard let himself out to open Emily's door. She avoided his eyes as she stepped out of the car. He followed her up the front steps.

When she turned around, he played Bogart again. "If that plane leaves the ground and you're not with him, you'll regret it. Maybe not today, maybe not tomorrow, but soon. And for the rest of your life."

Emily closed her eyes and smiled. "You'd better go," she whispered when she opened them.

The smell of her perfume caused him to linger for a moment before he turned to leave.

"Richard," she called after him.

He stopped.

"Dinner was lovely. Thank you."

He forced a smile.

Emily paused for a moment before she closed the door.

Richard held his head high on his walk back to the waiting limo. He slumped into the seat. *Let's hope you didn't blow it, Richard.* He second-guessed his decision to surprise her with the tickets. Perhaps it was too much too soon. Had he underestimated her recovery time? Would she recover?

He knocked on the privacy screen that separated the front and back seat. An electric motor whirred and the glass lowered.

"You got anything else to drink?" he asked the driver.

"There might be some Scotch in the—"

"I don't drink Scotch," he said to the eyes that watched him in the rearview mirror.

"You're probably better off," the driver said, eyes on the road again.

"How's that?"

"Mark Twain said, 'Too much of anything is bad, but too much good whiskey is barely enough.'" He turned from the road to the mirror. "Alcohol's not the answer."

"I suppose you know the answer?"

"I do."

"Care to enlighten me?"

He paused and their eyes met again in the mirror. "Life is a self-fulfilling prophecy."

Richard nodded. "Yeah, I've heard that one, but what does it mean?"

"I think you already know." The privacy screen rose.

Richard leaned forward and knocked on the glass. No response. He settled back into the seat and stared out into the night. The end of Casablanca played again in his mind. In the scene at the airport, Ilsa wanted Rick to board the plane with her, but he wouldn't go. The roles were reversed now. His story would end differently—they would be on that last plane out of Casablanca together.

CHAPTER **FIFTY-ONE**

Twice a week during the summer, local farmers offered produce for sale under several large tents in the parking lot of an empty building. Fresh fruit, vegetables and cut flowers were displayed on rows of folding tables. Emily, basket in hand, strolled down one of the aisles with Samantha at her side.

"What time does your flight leave?" Sam asked.

"Later this afternoon."

"Shouldn't you be packing?"

Emily inspected some tomatoes and placed two in her basket. "I'm not going."

"What?" Sam nudged her sister. "How could you pass up an opportunity like this?"

Emily tilted her head, eyes wide. "It's Richard, remember? I wouldn't want to be *naive* or anything."

"C'mon, Em, don't try to blame this on me."

"I told you. I want to feel like I'm the most important thing in his life again."

"Yeah, I remember." Sam rolled her eyes. "Good luck with that."

Samantha walked over to a bushel basket of peaches, picked one up, and took a bite.

Emily turned to scold her and noticed Richard's car drive by. The Blue Knight pulled into a parking space across the street. She wondered what Richard was doing downtown. Was he following her?

When the door opened and a stranger stepped out of the car, she handed her basket to Samantha. "Here, hold this."

"Where are you going?" Samantha stared slack-jawed as Emily ran across the street.

Emily confronted the stranger as he stood in front of a parking meter. "Excuse me. What are you doing?"

The man looked up. "Who's asking?"

"This is my husband's car," Emily replied, hands on her hips. "Why are you driving it?"

"I bought this car last week."

"Really?" This didn't make any sense. "Where?"

"From a friend. Richard Dunham."

"That's impossible."

"And you are…?"

"I'm his wife. I know him, and he would never sell this car."

The man folded his arms across his chest. "I'm sorry lady, but he did. Maybe you don't know him as well as you think you do."

She looked away while she tried to gather herself.

"I heard he had a pretty bad accident recently. Good thing for me he wasn't driving this car."

"Yeah. Good thing for *you*."

"If it's any consolation, he told me he needed the money to travel," the man offered. "Said he was going overseas."

Emily frowned. "Richard said that?"

The man nodded and dropped two coins into the meter. "Is it okay if I go now?"

She stared, lost in thought.

The man didn't wait for an answer.

"Delta Flight one-seven-three to Dublin will begin boarding in five minutes. Please have your boarding pass ready."

Richard stood and examined every face in the busy terminal. Again. Emily's wasn't among them. She'll be here, he thought. She has to be. Everything in his life had led up to this—the moment she walked into the terminal. The rest of their lives together depended on it.

Passengers boarded the plane, but still no Emily. Richard held his boarding pass in his hand and bit his lower lip as he scanned the faces coming and going. They called the next group of passengers. "Please, Em," he whispered.

When the last call was announced, he looked around one more time before heading for the jetway. He believed he'd done everything he could to convince Emily of his love and renewed commitment. He also believed that, however this played out, chance or coincidence would have nothing to do with it. If he ended up in Ireland alone, there would be a good reason for it. That, however, was not his intention.

The walk down the jetway grew more difficult with each step, and he turned around every few feet for another look. *Stop it. Have a little faith, man.* A flight attendant greeted him with a smile when he stepped onto the plane. A polite nod was all he could muster.

Richard inched down the aisle, forced to stop several times while passengers stowed their carry-on luggage in the overhead compartments. He checked his ticket against the numbers printed at the end of the rows until he found a match, then sat down next to the window. He glanced sideways at the empty seat next to him and then watched the last few passengers make their way from the front of the plane. Once again, Emily was not among them. His heart sank.

He watched through the window while the ground crew made the final preparations for take-off. Passenger activity on the plane decreased, and the crew began their final pre-flight preparations.

"Click... click..." The flight attendants made their way to the front of the plane, closing the overhead compartments. The sound reverberated in his ears.

"Excuse me," Richard said to one of them when she reached the end of his row. "Have they closed the doors yet?"

"No, but they will any minute now," she replied. "Is everything all right?"

"Yes." He lied. "How soon before we take off?"

"We should get underway in a few minutes." She smiled and continued up the aisle.

Richard attempted to adjust the air vent above his head before he focused his attention out the window. The empty baggage cars headed back toward the terminal. The plane moved, and he slumped a little lower in his seat. Another plane lifted off the tarmac and climbed into the low gray clouds.

The flight attendants pointed out the emergency exits and demonstrated the overhead oxygen masks. The plane pulled away from the terminal and taxied toward the runway while he watched their scripted performance.

He closed his eyes and thought about reaching for one of those masks.

CHAPTER **FIFTY-TWO**

Richard sat in the terminal at JFK International Airport with a single red rose on the seat beside him. He had a two-hour layover in New York City before he changed planes for the trans-Atlantic leg of his flight. The sheer number of people who passed through the terminal made him feel even more alone.

Emily should have come around by now and been on that plane. He pressed speed dial for Emily's cell and held the phone to his ear, not sure what he would say. A few seconds later, it didn't matter. Voicemail. He didn't leave a message. A more pressing question needed to be answered. Should he continue on to Ireland without her?

After twenty minutes of deliberation and two more attempts to reach Emily by phone, he made a decision—cancel the rest of the trip and book a flight back to Springfield. He would cut his losses, lick his wounds, and live to fight another day. He walked up to the ticket counter.

"Can I help you?"

"Hi. My name is Richard Dunham, and I wondered how I might—"

"Oh, Mr. Dunham," she interrupted. "I have a package for you."

Richard watched her bend down and reach under the counter. She stood and placed a large envelope in front of him.

Richard looked at the envelope and then back to the woman. "What's this?"

She shrugged. "I don't know. Someone dropped it off for you a few minutes ago. I was just about to have you paged to pick it up."

"Someone? What did they look like?"

"An older gentleman. Short. Gray hair."

"Did he leave his name?"

"No. He just said he was a friend and that you had left this behind." She pointed to the envelope. "He said it was important."

Richard picked up the envelope and stared at his name on the front. He thanked her.

"I'm so sorry, Mr. Dunham. I interrupted you." She smiled apologetically. "What was it you wanted to ask me?"

"Uh... never mind." He shook his head. "It can wait."

When he returned to his seat, he flipped the package over and squeezed the clasp. A large stack of papers, held together at the top by a metal binder clip, slid out onto his lap. He recognized his manuscript immediately—the manuscript he had written as Michael—but hesitated to believe his own eyes. A Post-It note was stuck to the title page. *This is your story, Son. With the right ending, it's sure to be a bestseller. Love, Dad.*

He lifted his head and scanned the gate area for any familiar faces. How was this even possible?

Slowly, he peeled back the cover sheet and looked at the words spread out across the page in neat little rows. Tens of thousands of them, and he remembered writing every one.

It needed a title. How does one sum up a lifetime of love and loss and emotional chaos in a few little words? It didn't seem possible at the time. It still didn't.

Richard thumbed through the pages, stopping from time to time to read a particular passage before he moved on. He thought about Michael's sister Angela. Was she real? Would their paths ever cross in this timeline? He could try to look her up, but what would he say to her?

About three-quarters of the way through the manuscript, a familiar voice spoke from somewhere behind him.

"Can I tell you a story, Rick?"

He froze, unsure whether the sound came from somewhere in the terminal or somewhere inside his head. Faith made him set the manuscript down and stand. He believed with all his heart that she would be there when he turned around.

Their eyes locked and time stood still. Richard cleared his throat and mustered up his best Bogart voice. "Does it have a wow finish?"

Emily slowly closed the space between them. "I don't know the finish yet," she said, her eyes as green as he'd ever seen them.

"Go on. Tell it. Maybe one will come to you as you go along."

They stood locked in each other's gaze. He searched those eyes until he found what he was looking for. The eyes don't lie.

Their lips met. Everything around them seemed to fade away. Their kiss was fueled by every embrace they'd ever shared.

When they came up for air, Richard took her hand and they sat. "How... how did you...?"

Emily smiled. "A magician never reveals her secrets." Her expression became serious. "I'm sorry, Richard. I should have—"

Richard placed his index finger to Emily's lips. "The only thing that matters now is that you're here."

"I don't know how you did it, but..." A grin broke out on her face.

He matched it with one of his own. "Richard 2.0."

Emily took a deep breath. "I still love you, Richard."

He made no attempt to hide the tear that slid down his cheek. He silently vowed to make sure nothing would ever change her mind. "What happened, Emily?" He searched her eyes. "When did we stop being us?"

Her expression softened. "Somewhere along the way we stopped communicating," she said. "I didn't know what you were thinking, and I feared the worst."

He realized that he'd shut her out. "That won't happen again. I've been—"

"I know. You've been telling me for the past two weeks, but I was the one who wasn't listening."

Richard held the rose between them.

Emily smiled. "What's this for?" She took it from him and held it below her nose.

"A new beginning." He watched her close her eyes and inhale. He paused until she opened them again and met his gaze. "The past is the past—"

She cut him off. "It's what we do next that matters."

An announcement interrupted their conversation. "Final boarding call for Delta flight 173 to Dublin."

Richard grabbed his manuscript from the seat. He could write the elusive ending now. He took hold of Emily's hand, and they walked together down the jetway.

"Does your boss accept unsolicited manuscripts?"

Emily raised an eyebrow. "Why? Are you thinking about writing a book?"

"Can I tell you a story, Emily?"

∞∞∞∞

A Note from the Author

Thank you for investing your valuable time in reading my novel. I hope you enjoyed the story. Please take a moment to visit **www.davidhomick.com** for more information about me and my books and to let me know what you thought of my story.

Word of mouth is the most powerful promotion any book can receive. If you enjoyed this book, please tell your friends, and consider writing a positive review on Amazon and Goodreads.

Other Books by David Homick

Broken Angels

Abandoned by his father as a child, Jack DiLuca cannot see that his self-destructive behavior and one-night stands are preventing him from finding the love and the life that he desires. Driven by recurring dreams about his father, he walks away from his first meaningful relationship to settle the score with the man who destroyed his life.

When Jack finds his father in Philadelphia, he discovers that everything is not as it appears. He gets more than he bargained for as family secrets are revealed, and he learns that even he is not who he thought he was.

A chance meeting with Maggie, an old high school flame, rekindles his desire, but she resists his attempts to get too close. After building a bond with her ten-year-old daughter, Jack longs to be part of a family. But when tragedy strikes, he discovers that Maggie hides a secret that threatens to destroy everything.

www.ingramcontent.com/pod-product-compliance
Lightning Source LLC
Chambersburg PA
CBHW021651110726

47902CB00007B/1920